# WEIGHT OF THE

# WORLD:

## THE PREQUEL

A D McCLOVER

**Weight of the World: the prequel**
Author: A D McClover
Cover Design by Jessica James Pro_Designx
Edited by Sharon Goodman
© Copyright 2016 by Dana Hanna

Centaur Publishing
www.CentaurPublishingCo.com

ISBN-13: 978-0997541717
ISBN-10: 0997541717

# Acknowledgements

First off, I want to thank God. For everything. The good and the bad. It all made me who I am today.

I want to thank Ms. Christine and Mrs. Mildred, my grandmothers and the first loves of my life. Mrs. Burnita, my mother, for raising a hard-headed, stubborn, hardworking son like me. RIP.

I love you Kevon and Savyen, my mini-mes. My two sons give me all the push I need to be great.

Also, I would like to thank Dana. I couldn't have done this without you. You saw something in me that I didn't even see in myself. Thanks for never candy-coating anything and always giving it to me raw. I love you.

I'd like to thank the guy on the cover, Mr. Stanley McClover. I got unconditional love for you. If you ever need me, I'm there for you.

I'd like to thank the lady on the cover, Jessica Johnson. I really, really appreciate the love and support. I owe you one! Oh, and congrats on your baby girl!

A special thanks to my homegirl, Angel Taylor. You took me to another level by just being yourself (even though you quit on me halfway through). I owe you big time. I appreciate you.

Shout-out to my favorite Facebook group, *Good Times*; everybody in there who fucks with me. Thanks for always letting me be me.

Last, but not least, I want to thank my whole family: Aunts, Uncles, Cousins. The McClover family. The Gibson family. Anybody who ever did me wrong. Anybody who ever did me right. Anybody who ignored me. Anybody who ever said, thought or wished I wouldn't make it.

And I gotta thank the city of Fort Lauderdale. You raised a tough kid who remembers the struggle. Thanks for the memories.

I knew all that college debt would be worth it one day!

*This book is dedicated to Christine, Mildred and Burnita - all the women I have loved and lost. RIP. Also, my future wife, Dana. I love you baby. Keep pushing me. I know I got more to give.*

# PROLOGUE

*I used to wonder why the game chose me...I'm just thinking to myself....*

It's the last day of my third year at Bethune-Cookman University and I was just as excited as I was my first day. I had almost completed a family dream; a college degree! Just one more year. College had been a life-altering experience for me. I left my grandmother's home at 17 years old, and was childish in a lot of ways. *"When I was a child, I spoke and thought and reasoned as a child. But when I grew up, I put away childish things."* That Bible verse comes to mind as I reminisce, because three years after I left home I felt like an adult because of the adult things I was doing. Between the girls, the drugs and the partying, I felt grown. Females always came easy to me. Talking to them, making them laugh, making them cry... I am my father's son! He died when I was five years old, but he left me with his DNA. I was a natural when it came to women. Most of them loved me, and the ones who didn't love me, didn't love themselves!

Fast forward to the drugs: I started selling at 15 and it was easy for me. I had a love affair with money; we were married. I never wanted for anything in middle school or high school. I took care of myself, but I felt the streets were always reeling me in. The streets welcomed everyone but had love for no one. It took me five years of blindness to finally see. I sold every kind of drug under the sun: weed, crack, coke, prescription pills, ecstasy—name it, I had it! And I was good at what I did. I thought I had found my calling! Scarface ain't have shit on me! Thousands of dollars every week at a young age. I was just 20 years old! I was seeing more money than I ever imagined, at that point in my life. I was the only one who could stop me and that's exactly what I did. I self-destructed. I got too comfortable. It was June 15th- about 6:30 in the morning when I decided to sell some ex pills and crack cocaine to an undercover police officer. And to add insult to injury, I was 1000 feet from a school zone, which turned my charge from a third-degree felony to a first-degree felony, punishable up to 15 years. Even though I had never been in any trouble as a juvenile, selling drugs in front of a school was considered one of the worst charges a person could get.

Things turned from sugar to shit in a matter of minutes. I went from top of the world to top of a bunk bed in Volusia

County Jailhouse. Things weren't looking good. All the money I was making couldn't save me from the damage I had done. I spent eight months in the county jail and spent thousands upon thousands of dollars on lawyers and legal fees; that still didn't save me from doing three years in prison. "We live and we learn," they say. Those 36 months changed my life. I began to look at life through bitter eyes. Twenty-one years old; I'd never been outside the state of Florida, never been away from my grandmother for longer than four months at a time, and just had a newborn baby boy. I went from making thousands of dollars some weeks to not even having two dollars to make a phone call to people on the streets who claimed they loved me and would be there for me! I might have wanted to say "Hello, happy birthday, how's everyone doing, I love you...." But I understand. Like my grandmother said, you made your own bed, now you have to lie in it!

But I still felt some type of way inside. For three years I turned my attention to self-preservation and figuring out who I wanted to be when I came home. I realized that once you turn eighteen, you're officially an adult and no one owes you *anything*. While incarcerated, I used my ears to hustle and soak up the game, and my pen to write down a plan. *Always the opportunist...*

**June 3**, three years later, the Department of Corrections opened the prison gates. I came out smarter than when I went in. I now had a three-year-old son, a five-year plan, and a head full of steam. I was never going to prison again. I had too much to do.

I was free!

# CHAPTER 1

## Part One: BUILDING BLOCKS

I been out of prison for 20 minutes. I'm now at the Greyhound bus station with one hundred dollars in my pocket, state-provided clothes and animosity on my mind because I been gone for three years with no help; no letters from nobody, no visits, nothing! I got a bus ticket with my choice to go anywhere that I chose in the US.

Fort Lauderdale- the place I was born and raised. My whole family was there: grandmas, cousins, aunts, uncles, friends, ex-girlfriends.... The history that I have in this city runs deep and I have too many ties there not to go back and not get any closure on that chapter in my life.

Seventeen hours later I get off the bus on Federal Highway in Ft. Laud. I'm finally home! First thing I do is kiss the ground, just thankful to have arrived safely. Now I need a phone and I need somebody to call. I walk to the front of the bus station where everybody is smoking cigarettes and I spot a young, white female on her phone. I wait for her to finish up her conversation.

"Excuse me ma'am...," I say to her, trying not to be rude or come off as aggressive. I know how some people would be instantly intimidated when approached by a dark chocolate, 6'4", 210lb stranger, "...but can I use your phone for a minute? I'm try'na call a ride to come and pick me up".

She froze for a minute, thought to herself for a second then, staring straight in my light brown eyes, said "Sure, you can use it."

I got the phone and dialed the first number that popped into my head. Grandma! My grandmother has always been good to me. In fact, she was good to all of her grandkids. Me and all my cousins grew up more like brothers and sisters, just how she wanted it. She gave me that lil' push I needed to get shit done. She demanded the utmost respect from everyone she came in contact with, without ever having to say a word. I knew, at a young age, that whenever that day came for me to walk down that aisle, my future wife would definitely have to have a lot of my grandma's qualities.

"Hey Ma, I just got out. I'm at the Greyhound station, can you come get me?"

My grandma started crying and screaming. That's how overjoyed she was that her favorite grandson was home.

"I'll be there in 20 minutes!" I heard her tell somebody in the background, "My baby Saint home! My baby Saint home!"

Right before I hung up the phone, out the corner of my eye, I caught the white girl looking at me. I hung up and handed it back to her.

"Thanks, I really appreciate it."

She replied with a smirk, "You're welcome. Anytime. So where you headed? It looks like you just got out."

"I did. About eighteen hours ago. I just did three years and I used that time to come up with a master plan. So, where *you* headed?"

"On my way to Miami to my sister's house. I'm trying to get my shit together myself!"

"Das wassup! So, what's your name?"

"My name's Amanda". She reached inside her purse, got out a pen and wrote down her phone number. "Call me when you get that master plan going." She chuckled a little, then, "So what they call you?" I gave her a little smirk as I opened my arms to give her a goodbye hug. As I was pulling away from the hug, I whispered in her ear: "They call me Saint. Me and you gon' be really good friends." Then

I walked away, and headed to my grandmother's car which had just pulled up. Before we drove away, I rolled down the window and yelled out:

"Remember my face. I'll be in touch."

# CHAPTER 2

Me and my grandmother fill the 20-minute ride home with small talk. She must have done a good job of distracting me because I didn't even notice all the cars in the yard. As I get out of the car, I hear everyone yelling, "Surprise!" Man, I'm shocked and mad at the same damn time, but I just slap a smile on my face and walk through the door. As I take a look around, I see not much has changed. It looks and smells almost exactly like it did the last time I was here, almost four years ago. It's sort of like potpourri, but my grandmother's own special blend. It always made everyone who walked in her door instantly feel at home. I drop my bag and give everyone hugs and kisses. Everyone is there: aunts, uncles, cousins, so-called friends…EVERYONE! All I see is teeth, all 32, from everyone I come in contact with.

For a split second, I almost forget how mad I am that everybody left me for dead for three years. "We miss you", "We love you", "We're so glad your home" …it *almost* feels genuine! I think that a lot of people are only capable of showing someone love when that person is right in front of them. The majority of the time, it's out of sight, out of mind.

As I make my rounds, making sure to greet everyone personally, I run into one of the last people on earth that I would have expected to be there. My son's mother. Immediately a range of emotions run through my body like a bolt of lightning. Anger, surprise, confusion; in my mind I'm thinking that this was supposed to be a "welcome home" celebration for people who love me, so why was she here? I was gone three years and she stopped writing me and putting money on the phone after six months. I don't even wanna look her in the face, but then I saw who she had with her; my first-born, my one and only child, my son, King. It wasn't even about me and her anymore, at least not at this moment. This was bigger than whatever we had going on.

He had changed a lot from the pictures she sent. He was only six months when she stopped writing, now he's three. Damn, he's gotten so big and he looks just like me. I did a good job! My heart softened instantly. It was love at first sight. I'd never felt like this about anyone before. He must have felt it, too, cause when I bent down to pick him up, he was staring me in the face the entire time. He laid his head on my shoulder and I could tell he knew that we were one and the same. I didn't let him outta my arms until he fell asleep, hours later. This was also my family's first time meeting him, but me and him needed this little bonding time. I refused to let anyone else hold him that night. It was my and his first day of many to come. So after he fell asleep in my arms, around eleven o'clock, I laid him in the bed and got back to the party.

As I'm walking down the hall, I really take it all in. I look around at all the memories in my grandmother's home. She was sort of a hoarder, because she kept every picture of every grandchild that she was ever given. She kept every award we received, every Mother's Day gift we ever gave her. She kept everything! She loved her family. I spotted a baby picture of me on the wall. King looked exactly like me. We were identical. I think to myself, *I gotta do better for him.* I go back into the main room where everyone was mingling. Now I could focus on seeing where my son's mother's head was. I hadn't spoken to her nor received a letter from her in two and a half years. I felt betrayed. I needed closure.

# CHAPTER 3

Lashonda Wallace, my child's mother...

She still looked as good as she did when we first met in college, maybe even a lil' better, but I wasn't big on small talk these days, especially with her. I was furious.

"Hey Saint," she said, smiling from ear to ear. But she saw the look on my face and she knew I wasn't happy. We were together for two years in college, so she knew me pretty well.

"I missed you, baby daddy!" No comment. I wasn't playing with her. "I know you mad at me. I'm sorry. I ain't never been with anybody who went to prison before. I ain't know what to do or how to handle it. It was hard out there while you were gone. I'm just being honest." Something she said made me look her dead in the eye and almost shed a tear. All the disappointment and frustration that I had for her faded away once I realized the predicament that I had left her in. But I still had to talk to her firm, that's the only way she listened to me, "What the fuck made you think I knew what to do or how to handle it? You act like I been to prison before! You were one of the last people that I put my faith in and you let me down. I used to love you, man! You disappointed me." I had to put my foot down. Not too hard, but hard enough to let her know that what she did wasn't right. We were in love before I went and did my bid, and she said she was gonna be right by my side the whole time. She lied. She started to cry, but my heart wasn't really on feeling sorry for anybody at that time. So I looked away, talking to her, but with my back turned, "So what happened to everything I left you? I left you over twenty-five thousand dollars. I left you three cars, I left you all of my jewelry, clothes, shoes…Lashonda! I left you my heart! What happened?" It wasn't time for me to hold anything back because more than likely, this was gonna be our last time having this conversation. I needed to get everything off my chest NOW. She began to cry even louder. I eventually turned around to face her because I like to see people's expressions when they've done me wrong. "So you don't have an answer? You don't have nothing to tell me? After two years and a child together, I feel like I deserve SOME kind of explanation. So…who is he?" I let that last question hang in the air like a kite.

"Who are you talking about?" She wasn't crying anymore, but her eyes were still wet.

"Who's the dude you left me for? Do I know him? I wanna be able to leave you with a clear conscience." Her body language gave it away. She shifted from side to side uncomfortably, and that was a dead giveaway. I studied psychology in college so I knew how to read body language, and I'm sure she knew that. After a couple of minutes of looking everywhere, except in my eyes, I guess she came to the conclusion that she was gonna just tell me the truth.

Head down to the ground, she said, "I spent it. All your clothes and shoes I gave to my brothers. I sold the cars. I was out here by myself and shit was hard and I needed help! I had a newborn baby!" Now my head dropped to the ground. I was really torn about what she had to go through for our child. Then she dropped another bomb. "And you were right, while you were gone, I had got me a lil' friend and we been messing around the whole time...." I wasn't really surprised. But what she *did* surprise me with, is when she told me who it was. "...and it's Rico." I said, "Rico WHO?" She said, "Your roommate from college. I'm so sorry, it just happened Saint, he reminded me so much of you. And now it's too late to turn back cause we in love." I gave her a look that said *'you dirty bitch'*. Then I told her, "I appreciate your honesty, but out of all the men in the world, you chose one of my best friends? I would have never done that to you." And I really meant that. I know I ain't have a squeaky clean record; I did my dirt too, but I would have never had sex with her friend. Damn! I thought everyone knew that some lines were not supposed to ever be crossed.

All I could do was shake my head in disappointment. It was then that I realized that shit was real. It was time for me to put on my big boy pants and close that chapter of my life for good. Now, my only goal was to take care of my son and be involved in his life as much as possible, cause his mother done ruined any chance of us ever reuniting. Now, I wouldn't piss on her if she was on fire. We finished!

# CHAPTER 4

New days bring new adventures….

I been home from prison like a week already. I resolved that situation with my son's mother. I couldn't possibly stay mad at her for everything that she'd done, hell, I wasn't exactly loyal myself, to be honest. So I got over it in my heart, but I knew that we would never be together again. She also confessed to me that she didn't get rid of *everything*. She kept my truck. A few days after the "welcome home" party, she dropped it off to me and said goodbye. That chapter is now officially closed. Even though everything that I lost while I was gone for them three years was just things, they were *my* things! But I'm over that now.

As the days go by, I been running into family and friends who I felt were against me, as well. The first relative that I ran into since my coming home party was my cousin Doug. Me and Doug always been close. We grew up more like brothers. So for me to say that I think highly of him is an understatement.

"Saint, cuz, I'm glad I caught you by yourself! You got a few minutes? You think we can go somewhere and talk?" He caught me by the corner store near the house. I had to think about it cause, in actuality, I had cut my cousin Doug loose. He happened to be a casualty of war and he didn't know it yet, but since we were once close like brothers, I decided to give him a few minutes of my time. "What's up? Make it quick, I got shit to do!" His first statement to me was, "First off, what's the attitude for?" In my head, I thought he must have lost his damn mind! So I ignored him. Then he said, "Well anyways, since you been home you ain't really acting like the old you. It seems like you don't fuck with me no mo'? I left you my number at the party, you ain't never call me. What's that all about?" It took me a couple seconds to make sure the right words came out my mouth. "What you mean acting like the old me? I *ain't* the old me! I just did three years in prison and wasn't nobody there for me like I needed them to be. And it ain't that I don't fuck with you no mo', that ain't it. I ain't fuckin wit *nobody* no mo'. One-man show. And you're right, you did leave me your number at the party, now my only question is how the fuck was I gon' call you wit no phone? That's the shit I be talkin' bout! Ya'll don't think out here in these streets. Buy me a phone if you want me to call you!" In my mind, I already knew these dudes wasn't thinking on my level. He looked surprised, like he ain't known me his whole life and said, "You dead right cuz." He reached into his pocket and gave me everything he had in it. He stood in front of me and handed it to me. "I'm not sure how much this is, but this should be close to four thousand dollars. I spent a couple hundred, but this for you, cuz. And you right bout everything you said. I'm sorry about everything. This might not make it all better, but this a good start. I love you cuz, I'm sorry." No matter how mad I was at my cousin Doug, I had too much love for him not to accept his apology and his money. And that probably was all I really needed all along. "I love you too, cuz." We gave each other a hug and he wrote his number down for me again. He laughed and said, "Now you got enough money to buy twenty phones. Call me cuz, we gotta link up on some biz." I told him, "I got you cuz. Appreciate it."

# CHAPTER 5

Two down and a couple more to go!

Now that I got a few grand in my pocket, I can breathe a lil'! I ain't looking for nobody in particular to vent my frustration on, but if we run into each other, it's goin' down. It's not in me to feel a certain way about a situation and not let it be known. Before I got locked up, I had plenty of friends and girlfriends. Everybody loved me, or so I thought! When my friends needed to borrow money, they came to me. If they needed food to eat, I made sure their stomachs were full. When they needed a place to stay until they got on their feet, my door was always open. I guess people have different definitions of the word friend.

**July 6th** I logged onto Facebook, just to see what the word on the street was...being nosey! I see all the females that I used to be in some sort of relationship with before I went to prison. Lo and behold I look on my Facebook wall and all I see is "FREE SAINT", "We miss you Saint", "We can't wait for you to come home Saint", "I love you Saint". But if all of this is true, why I never received a letter? No money. No visits. Nothing! But really I cared more about those letters. Those letters would have made my day. When the deputy called your name and put those letters on your bed, it made your time in jail not seem so bad...for that one day. And I would re-read the same letters over and over again. That was the beauty of a letter, words on a phone were different from a person being able to read certain paragraphs and sentences multiple times and using your own imagination to try and figure out what mind frame they were in when they wrote it. Too bad I didn't receive many. While I'm on Facebook, I see my message box blinking. I click it and the first message I see is from one of the women that had a piece of my heart; *Talia*, my Puerto Rican princess. I was still mad at her too, though. Even though she knew that I was in a relationship with Lashonda, that never stopped anything that me and her had going on. I read her message in my inbox.

"Hey Saint, I miss you bae. I wish you were here with us. Us, meaning me and your son. Yes, I said your son. His name is Zion. He's one now and whenever you get out, call me so that I can introduce you to him. I found out I was pregnant shortly after you got locked up. My number is 772-441-5538. I moved back to New York but I'll be down there to see you when you get out. I love you." I looked at the date on the message and it's dated February 12ᵗʰ two years earlier.

Wow! Another son born the same year from a second woman! I really need to slow down. More responsibility and another mouth to feed. I ain't got no problem with that. If I was man enough to make him, I'm damn sure gonna be man enough to take care of him! I need to call her, but first, let me go on her Facebook page and see if this lil' boy look like me. He does! I called the number two minutes after I saw Zion's picture.

# CHAPTER 6

Ring ring ring...

"Hello, can I speak to Talia?"

"This her, who this?" she replied, somewhat sounding like she recognized my voice. "This Saint. Wassup, baby mama?" It was straight silence on the phone for a good ten seconds. "Oh, my God!!! When did you come home?" All I hear is crying. "I been home for bout a month, but I just got your message on 'the Book' bout twenty minutes ago". She told me, "I know you were surprised by the message I left you, but I just had to tell you. I couldn't keep it a secret. I'm sorry for waiting so long, I was scared. I ain't know what to do!" Now I was silent. I ain't know what to say. "He got my eyes and my ears, but he got yo' color". I hesitated. "No disrespect, I know we did our thang together for a couple of years or whatever, but, are you sure he's mine? I'm just asking!?" It took her about ten seconds, which seemed like ten minutes to say, "Saint, as much as we loved each other, do you think I'd ever do you like that?" I immediately answered, "No. No I don't. So what do we do from here?" She said, "You tell me. You used to keep an answer for every question…you remember what you told me when we first met when we was in the 9ᵗʰ grade? You said 'let me do the thinking for both of us'. And from that moment on, I knew you was a man that would always have an answer and that always knew where he was going, and if you led the way, I'd follow. So *you tell me*, what's next?" It ain't take me long to realize she was right; she'd known me for a long time. So I replied, "I need you to get on the next flight down here, you and my son, so that I can see ya'll." Then she hit me with, "What flight? I moved back down to Broward County six months ago. I got my own place in Coral Springs. You can come over when I get off work at six o'clock tomorrow. That cool?" I told her, "You know that's cool. I'm gon' fuck wit ya tomorrow." We said our goodbyes and hung up the phone. Shit is starting to come together…

# CHAPTER 7

Now that things are starting to look up for me, I think it's time for me to start letting go. For me, it's easier to love than to hate. And at the end of the day, all I really wanna do is see my kids grow up together, and for me to provide them with everything that I never had. They're my motivation.

I got a couple of hours before meeting my son, Zion, for the first time. I already got my other son, King, with me. We on our way to Coral Square Mall to shop for some learning supplies for them. Maybe grab them both one of those Leapfrog kid's tablets and some flash cards or something. I need them to be ten steps ahead of all the other kids. While we were in the mall, I ran into an old friend that I haven't seen since middle school...Vince.

"Hey Vince. Wassup homie? Long time, no see!" He had gained some weight since I last saw him, maybe about thirty pounds, but other than that, he still looked almost the same. Only now, he has long dreadlocks hanging down to the middle of his back. We gave each other a hug. He was smiling, "Saint! What's up, my boy? Long time is right. At least ten years! Damn! You ain't aged a bit. How you do it?"

All I could do was smile and shrug my shoulders, "I don't know! I been drinking out the fountain of youth, I guess!" We both laughed.

Me, Vince and King walked to the food court to grab something to eat. While we're sitting, he started telling me that he'd made a couple of bad decisions in his life. He didn't go into detail, but he did mention that he'd gotten out of prison recently.

"Saint, lemme ask you something? What do you think about going back to school and taking up a trade or something?" Actually, I have thought about it. But I wasn't quite sure if now was the time. He went on, "The government will pay for whatever you decide to take up. In other words, SCHOOL'S FREE!" The word 'free' always intrigued me because free wasn't always really free. I would have to sacrifice *something*. I guess he saw me struggling with this in my head, cause before I could answer, he said, "Just think about it." He took a card out of his pocket and handed it to me. "Check 'em out!"

We sat there eating and talking for a little while longer, exchanged numbers, then he said he had to leave. *"Planting seeds…,"* that's what he left with me. I sat there while King finished up and was thinking about what Vince said. I'd been cutting hair since I was eight years old. I wouldn't mind getting my barber's license. Even though cutting hair wasn't the same kind of money that I was used to making, it was still better than doing something stupid and risking going back to prison. I know one thing: it was time for me to try something new. Because whatever I was doing before, obviously wasn't working out too well cause I still ain't made it rich yet. I know my kids are depending on me and they don't even know it yet. So at that moment, my mind was made up, I was going to school.

But right now, it was time for my two sons to be introduced to each other. I hopped on the phone and called Zion's mother.

"Wassup, baby mama? You home yet?"

"I just got home. You on your way here?"

"Yeah, and I got King wit' me too. I bought them some books and some other things...I want them to chill with each other and really get to know each other, they brothers."

She said, "I know. He's welcome here. I'm home and we're waiting on ya'll."

"Alright. We leaving the mall now, I'll be there in about twenty minutes." I had everything mapped out. I was starting from the top to the bottom, and at the top was my kids. The bottom was everything else. Since I grew up without a father, I already knew what it felt like to not have one around. So I had to do better.

# CHAPTER 8

Forty minutes later, I arrive at Talia's house. She lives in a pretty nice neighborhood, I'm impressed. I pull up in front and put the truck in park. I turn to face King, who is in the car seat on the back passenger side. I had to let him know what was going on. He's looking at me with those big, brown eyes and asking, "Where are we Daddy?" I smiled at him, "King! I got a surprise for you!" I wait for his face to light up, he loves the word 'surprise'. "You have a little brother and we're going to meet him." He takes the news of having a brother better than I did. He's smiling and clapping, "I got a bwudder, Daddy?"

"Yeah man. You got a brother and we're gonna see him right now. You ready?" He almost jumps out the car seat! He's ready. I unbuckle him and grab a few of his toys from off the back seat. I grab the bag of things that I got at the mall and get out the car. I open the back door and take him out, grab his hand and walk to the front door. He's singing the whole time, "I got a bwudder, I got a bwudder!!" When we get to the door, I let him knock. His knocks are soft, but loud enough for Talia to hear. He looks up at me for approval. I praise him, "Good job. That's my big man!" He's smiling from ear to ear. Then Talia yells out, "Coming!" I haven't seen her in over three years. I wonder if she's still sexy. But that's a story for a different day; today was about my boys. A few seconds later the door opens. Yep! Still sexy! Then I look down and see this tiny, curly-haired little boy, that looks just like King! King is looking at him like he knows, as well. I ain't waste any time in saying, "Yeah! He mine!" I knew instantly. Everybody was smiling and hugging each other; me, Talia, King and Zion. After I let go of Talia, I pick up King, then Zion at the same time. I look them both in the face, with a small tear in the corner of my eye, and say, "I'm your daddy and ya'll are brothers. I love both of ya'll very much." Talia stands by as I hold my sons. I know that I need to be there for them. They need me, and I need them too!

I want to catch up with Talia, so I put the boys down and let them go in the room to play with their new things. Me and Talia sit down on the couch and caught up on some of the time we'd lost. As we're catching up, I couldn't help but notice that she dyed her hair- added some blonde highlights or something. It looks nice. I get flashbacks of our middle school days when we first started messing around. We'd been together, off and on, for so long, that I'd taken for granted how fine she is. She has her nose pierced now. I guess a lot has changed since college. She's wearing my favorite Miami Dolphins jersey with a pair of white booty shorts that she knows will turn me on. She ain't slick! She must be tryin' to make another baby! I look back to see what the boys are doing. They're busy playing with their trucks and cars; making all types of *"vroom vroom"* noises, and so forth. Damn! I got two sons now. It still didn't fully sink in.

Back to Talia...I ask her about Zion. How is he doing in pre-school? How does he act? Does he have any of my traits? She says," Of course, he's just like you." I even ask about her life and what she has going on. She told me she has a friend, but nothing serious. For a second, I was just as mad at her as I was at Lashonda. Then Zion called me over to come play...fuck it! *This* is why I came here, right? I get up and go into the other room with my boys...vroom vroom....

# CHAPTER 9

An idle mind is the Devil's playground...

That's why I keep my mind busy. I know that I can be a procrastinator, and it's very hard to hold my attention for more than ten minutes, so it was kind of difficult when I woke up Monday morning to keep my mind set on signing up for school. But I went on down to the Florida Academy of Beauty in Ft. Lauderdale and signed up for the barber's course; a course that I knew I could finish. I been home from prison a little over 30 days and already the pressure is starting to build...but it's good pressure. I got both of my kid's moms rooting for me and praying for me to do well because they knew that the better they child's father did, the better the kids will do. All they want from me is to stay free and be a good provider for my two little boys.

After I signed up for school, I figured I needed a little more grounding, and someone from the outside to help guide me in this path of life that I'm choosing. I chose a woman I've known and respected for at least six years. I even called her "Ma", because she was definitely like a mother figure to me since my own mother passed not too long before I went to prison. Her name was Mrs. Bennett and she only lived ten minutes from me, so I decided to just pop up at her house, even though that's not like me. But I did it anyways. *Knock, knock, knock*...ten seconds later she yells out, "I'm coming." She sounds like she was waiting on somebody. "It's Stephon", I yell through the door, knowing that she would be really, really happy to see me. She always is. You know she had to be someone special in my life for me to use my government name. She was the only one allowed to call me that. Then I hear her yell, "Oh my God!!! Son! Son, is that really you?" I could just see her smiling now. She's not my real mother, but you couldn't tell her that! "Yeah, it's me Ma. I haven't seen you in a while, just stopping by to chat wit' you for a few." She tells me to give her two seconds.

During those supposed two seconds she took to come to the door, I use the time to go over in my head what I'm gonna say. She finally opened the door and she's smiling from ear to ear. You can sense that there is genuine love and happiness to see me. "Hey son!" she says, as she gives me a big hug. "Hey Ma!" I say, soaking in all of the affection. After she lets me go, she asks me, "So, what brings you by today?" I say, "I didn't know I needed a reason to stop by and see my favorite lady in the whole wide world. You look just as beautiful as the last time I saw you!"

"Always the charmer", she says, smiling widely. "You always know how to make me feel special. I heard about your little *vacation*. Good to have you back home."

I begin, "I actually stopped by because I need your opinion about a situation. I don't value too many people's opinions, but yours just happens to be one of the few that I do." She told me to come inside and have a seat on the couch. "What's going on, baby? What's on your mind?"

"Well, I've been out for over a month and I've decided to go back to school to get my barber's license. I need to know if this is the right time to start school and commit fully to this situation. I'm also trying to stay out of jail, so I'm not try'na sell drugs anymore. Can you help guide me in the right direction?" She smiled and said, "Well son, I've been wanting to have this conversation with you for a couple of years now...." She smiled and sipped her cup of coffee. I sat with my legs crossed, waiting for her to answer. "You are a very intelligent and educated young man who has the world at his feet. You see different angles and can read people's body language and you can put together words effortlessly, and that's a blessing in itself. So, in my opinion, you've gotta do something with that gift of gab that you have. I see you as being great, not mediocre. Now, as far as school, that's a start for a lot of people at a lot of different times in their life. I just don't see school at this exact moment in time for *you*." I was nodding my head in agreement, because I, too, always saw great things for me. She continued, "Now, I'm not telling you to go back to selling drugs. What I'm saying is use your gift!" I told her to repeat that last part. "USE YOUR GIFT". One little tear rolled down the corner of my left eye. Those were the best three words anyone had ever told me, up to this point. Immediately I got up, wiped that tear from my eye, gave her a big hug and thanked her. While I was sitting in my truck in her driveway, it came to me what she meant by those three words. Time to take flight! It was time to take it to another level.

# CHAPTER 10

I found myself at home packing a small suitcase. It's not like I had a lot of things anyway, thanks to Lashonda. But anyway, I had my mind set. I was on my way to Miami to see what's up with my little friend from the bus stop, Amanda. The first thing I needed to do was to call her and see what she had goin' on. It's been several weeks since I'd seen her. She was the first name and person to pop in my mind after I left Ma's house. Truthfully, she was one of the few names I had saved in my phone. Ring ring ring...she picked up. "Hello?" She sounded like she was half asleep. "What's up Amanda?" I said it in a way that made it seem like we've known each other forever, even though this was the first time she'd ever heard my voice over the phone. "Who's calling?" she said, sounding more awake now. "This Saint", I said. "Do you still remember me? I hope you ain't forget about me already." She ain't sound asleep no more!

"Man! I been waiting for you to call me for weeks now! You gon' live a long time, I swear I was just talking about you yesterday!" She started laughing. "So wassup stranger? The last time we talked, you said something about getting your master plan together. You musta got everything together now?" I loved the fact that she remembered our brief conversation, that must mean I left some kind of impression on her. So I replied like only I could reply, "You know if you fail to plan, then you ultimately plan to fail. But listen, if I tell you a duck can pull a truck, shut the fuck up and hook it up! Let me do the thinking for both of us!" I said all of this with a straight face, by the way. I came at her like that for three reasons: 1. I wanted to get a reaction from her...check out her personality. 2. I was actually trying to make her laugh. Laughter always breaks the ice. And 3. I was subliminally trying to let her know that if she followed me, I wouldn't lead her wrong. She should trust what I say, even if it sounds far-fetched. Every move I make has to be calculated, and all of my words have to be carefully and strategically thought out. It apparently worked, she burst out laughing and said, "OK then! I know that's right! A man with a plan! So, answer me this, when am I gonna see you again?" She took the words right out my mouth. I knew this was the right girl from the moment we met. I answered, "That's an easy one...when do you wanna see me?" I had to keep it smooth. I couldn't sound too anxious. Females don't like thirsty, needy dudes and that will *never* be me.

Without skipping a beat, she said "Shit! I'm free right now!" PERFECT response! I told her, "Well, text me the address, I'm on the way!"

The journey of a thousand miles starts with the first step…those words keep replaying in my head. I hang up the phone, grab my keys, grab some cash and grab my suitcase. Off to Miami, Dade county I go! And if everything works out, hopefully I won't be coming back. At least not to live. I'll call my grandma when I get to where I'm going. Hell, I don't even really know where that is yet….

# CHAPTER 11

This lil' thirty minute drive that it's gon' take me to get to her sister's house in North Miami is all the time I'll need to map out my next few steps with Amanda. One thang's for sho', two thangs are for certain, and three thangs are a guarantee, that if you stay ready you ain't gotta get ready; I believe in that motto. It just sounds like it fits me. It sounds like it was made for me, as a matter fact I'm mad that I ain't think of it myself! But anyways, I really didn't know what I was gon' say to her when I got there, but I was confident it would come natural. I started laughing to myself like, "Saint, boy, you really finna go through wit' it, ain't no turning back now." My mama always told me that if I was gonna do something in life, be the best at it. Between my brains and her beauty, why wouldn't we make a perfect match? I mean, females have always been drawn to me since elementary school. I think they just like a man with a plan; a man that's going somewhere. A female doesn't mind following a good leader. I know it don't make no sense for *both* of us to be out here in these streets lost. In actuality, I don't really have a master plan per se, but what I do have is a will. And where there's a will, there's a way! Money was most definitely the motivation. I got off of I-95 South, exit of North Miami, in the right-hand lane, heading west. I look at my GPS with her address on it and it says I'm five minutes away. So as I'm heading west I stop by this 24-hour liquor store, grab a fifth of Patron and two cups, then get back en route. The GPS is now indicating that I have arrived at my destination, so while I'm sitting downstairs in her parking lot, I pop open the Patron, fix me and her a cup, and I tell myself, *If you stay ready, you ain't gotta get ready.* Then I dial her number. Ring ring ring…. "Hey Saint you here?" she says, sounding excited. "Yeah I'm downstairs. Pack a bag with some overnight clothes," I said. Then she replies, "OK I'll be down in five minutes." No questions asked, she hangs up the phone. It's on!

# CHAPTER 12

All the animosity and anger that was inside me when I first got out fell to the wayside. It takes too much time and energy to focus on people that wasn't there for me, I re-focus on the people who are there for me *now*. And that's starting with Amanda. This whole little endeavor that me and her finna encounter has very little to do with me and her having sex. Matter of fact, sex is the furthest thing from my mind. I'm try'na make a mental and spiritual connection.

Amanda comes downstairs with her overnight bag and gets in on the passenger side and the first thing she does is give me a hug and a kiss on the cheek. She's a classic beauty; blonde hair, blue eyes, 5'6", mid-C cup breast. She reminds me of the cheerleaders from high school; the girl-next-door type. She has on a pair of cut-off jean shorts and a tight white tank top. "Hey Papi," she looks down at the armrest and says, "is this cup for me?" She starts smiling. "Of course it is. This is just a little somethin' to set the vibe", I said, smiling. "So what you got on your mind, boo?", she said. I begin, "You intrigue me. I just wanna get to know you a little bit. Do you have kids? Where are your parents? Any more brothers or sisters?" These questions were just laying the foundation for certain things I needed to know before we take it to the next level. She wasn't timid, nor did it seem like she minded being put on the spot. It almost felt like she had this conversation before, she was real comfortable. While I wait for her to answer, I watch her demeanor. She doesn't fold her hands across her chest in a defensive position, nor does she look away like she's embarrassed by the questions I was asking her. She looks directly at me when she starts to speak, "Well...a little about myself. Let's see...," she pauses so she can put together the right words or to figure out how much she really wants to tell me, "I'm twenty-seven years old, Chicago born and raised. I have one sister, she's four years older than me and, as you already know, that's who I'm staying with right now. I came down here from Chicago because things weren't going too good. Our mom passed away about six years ago. The police found her with a needle in her arm. They said she overdosed from heroin, but she had been doing drugs for the past ten, fifteen years and we knew she only did enough just to get herself through the day. Our stepdad, Mitch, turned her out. They did drugs together. He had her prostituting to support their habit. So, me and my sister basically raised ourselves. The only person that loved and really cared about me was my sister." She stopped for a moment and I kept silent, waiting for her to say more. "And, that's why I don't do drugs. I experimented a tiny bit in high school, but I like to keep a clear head and be in control of any situation that I'm in." Now she has me curious, "You said you and your sister raised yourselves, so what did ya'll do for money?" I could guess what they did, but why would I assume; she's sitting right in front of me and, apparently, she don't mind telling! "Well, we used to dance at different strip clubs in the area. We did that for a few years. We even saved enough money to buy a car!" I like this girl already. She's not shy, but I can tell that she's holding something back. "Is that *all* ya'll did?" She knows what I'm asking. "Truthfully, I did whatever I had to do. But my sister would only dance. Sex was just business to me. I never catch feelings. In Chicago, there were men in every club trying to make me and my sister work for them. They even threatened us, that's why she left and came to Florida. It took me a little longer to get here." She just stared at me for a second. "You remind me of my stepdad. Ya'll look alike. You ever been to Chicago?"

"Nah, I never been out of Florida. So, what happened to Mitch?"

"Oh, Mitch? The police found ol' Mitch stabbed to death about four days after they found my mom." Her voice kind of trailed off as she said the last part, and she wasn't looking in my eyes anymore. Now she was just looking into space. That's enough for one day, we'll finish this later. I know all I need to know right now! I ask her, "Ready to take a ride with me?" I needed to break the silence and it seemed like she needed a moment. "Sure", she said. I put the truck in Drive and we headed to nowhere in particular. The radio was on, the windows were down and we were just riding, no talking, just enjoying the peacefulness.

We rode down Miami Beach, Aventura, Bal Harbor and Star Island. I would point out the big, nice mansions and homes along the way, so she could see how the big boys live. Almost like a version of reverse psychology. While in Bal Harbor I stopped in front of this mini-mansion, this house had to cost at least 5 million. I rolled down her window and pointed it out. "What you think about that?" I let the question hang in the air for a few seconds. "Love at first sight...a dream come true", she said. I think this is a good time to pick up the conversation we started an hour back. "Where do you see yourself in five years? I'm just try'na see if we're heading in the same direction." She thought to herself for about two minutes, like I had asked her a life-altering question. "I never really thought about it. You know what... that's a good question and I don't even have an answer for you. How about I got a better question for *you*," she said with a kind of serious face. "What's the question?"

She asked, "Where do *you* see me in five years?" with a twinkle in her eyes that I've never seen before. "I see you goin' as far as you let me take you." I paused, then said, with a straight face like I've been talking like this forever when actuality it just started flowing out of me, "We shootin' for the stars and if we come up short, we still gon' land on the moon, baby girl." She started smiling and said, "Well call NASA and tell 'em we comin'!" She then said, "I believed in you the minute I met you. Now I need to know what you need me to do for the team, *our* team, because I see the big picture."

"We gon' get that mansion within 12 months, but what I need you to do is let me do the thinking for the both of us, I just need you to trust me. Can you do that for me?" She said, "I wouldn't be here with you right now if I didn't." She looked me in my eyes and said, "Let's go get it papi, what I gotta do?"

# CHAPTER 13

## Part Two: PLAN INTO ACTION

I'm on I-95 heading north, on my way to wherever the wind blows. I got $2700 and a dream. Amanda got five dollars, a pack of Newports, an overnight bag and a head full of ambition. I was thinking about going up north, to maybe Georgia, first. I wanted to know how she felt about it, because all the decisions that I'm gonna hafta make, I'm gon' make it my business to include her in 'em as well. So I ask her, "What do you think about Atlanta for a few weeks or so, then we head a little further west?"

"I wouldn't mind going to Atlanta. I've never been there. Then we can go wherever afterwards" she says, sounding enthusiastic. Now that I know I got her, I figure this would be a good time to see how she feels about the plan.

"This is what we gonna do when we get there; first we gon' find the strip club that makes the most money. We gon' get you a job, we gon' buy you your outfits for work and you gon' work there for a couple weeks and you gon' be all that you can be. We gon' get us a nice room at the 'W'." This is my first time actually revealing some parts my plan to her, so I'm waiting for her reaction. "We a team papi! You lead, I follow. I like how you think. And I know one thing, I'm tired of being broke," she says, looking me directly in my eyes. "Well bae, I ain't never been broke. I don't even hang around broke people. The only thing a broke dude can teach me is how to be broke with him. We already rich." And I looked her right in her eyes and said, "Repeat after me...we already rich." With her chin held up high, she said, "We already rich. Yeah! We already rich papi!" I see that twinkle in her eye again.

# CHAPTER 14

Downtown Atlanta 1:17 AM, we're here!

I pull up at the 'W'. This not my first time here but I know it's hers. If I'm gonna sell her on the dream of the good life and the hope of better things to come, it should start where we lay our heads. It's obvious that she's impressed, she doesn't have to say a word, her eyes tell it all.

I put the truck in Park, but keep the engine running. I look over at her and tell her, "I'll be right back. I'm gonna go check us in." Trying to conceal her excitement, the only words she can muster is "Ok. "She doesn't even look my way, she's still looking around at how big and bright and pretty everything is. Now, this is actually only my second time here, but I have to make it seem like it's nothing new to me.

I hop out my truck and go to the front desk. The receptionist has her back to me, so at this point, all I can see was her long, straight black hair. When I ring the bell, I don't know what to expect when she turns around. I must have scared her because she turns around real fast and puts her hand up to her chest. "Excuse me ma'am, I didn't mean to scare you." *Damn, she fine!* She's tall, just how I like 'em, and has that exotic kinda look. I need her. "Ooh! You caught me off guard!" She says, catching her breath. She is beautiful. I'm sure she feels me staring at her. We lock eyes for about five seconds before I say, "I'm sorry. How are you doing tonight? I love your hair, by the way. It's so black and it moves like silk. I bet it feels like silk, too." I do a quick look-over without being too obvious. She is young, about my age; early-twenties and not quite as shy as she puts on to be. She has that long, black hair, light brown eyes, about 5'10", nice shape and about the same 'C' cup as Amanda, with a pecan complexion. I gather all of this info about her in about fifteen seconds, those psych classes are really paying off.

She replies with the biggest country smile on her face, "I'm doing well, and thank you for noticing." She's blushing and instinctively runs her fingers through her hair. Whenever a woman shows you all thirty-two teeth in the first five minutes, there's something that needs to be explored. Still smiling, she asks, "And how may I help you tonight, sir?"

"Well I need a room for tonight with one king size bed", I say. Then she says, "Give me just one second", she types on her computer for about a minute then says, "You're in luck, we have two rooms left. There's one on the 18th floor overlooking downtown Atlanta. Would you like it?"

"Yes ma'am I would," I said. "You can call me Trish. I'm not old enough to be a ma'am," she says blushing, trying to hide the dimple in her left cheek. She turns around to get some paper for the printer and as she stands on her toes reaching for the top shelf, I see more of her shape. She had a nice, slim figure with extra-long legs. That work uniform doesn't do her body any justice, but that skirt goes perfectly with those hips. *Snap out of it Saint!* She turns back around and catches me looking, but I wasn't trying to hide my interest. I want her. "Excuse me, Trish, I don't mean to be nosey, but I hear a l'il accent. Where are you from?"

She smiles again, "I'm from Guyana. Do you want to know how much the room is per night?" She waits for a response.

"Trish, if I hafta ask how much the room is, then I probably can't afford it." I flash her my million-dollar smile, as if to say *you should've known better than to ask me a question like that.* "You're right I'm sorry," she says, almost embarrassed. "It's cool Trish, but don't be sorry, be yourself." I am smiling because I know I almost have her. "You too pretty to be sorry."

*Now that might've closed the deal,* I say to myself. She starts smiling from ear to ear. She's kind of shy, looking at the ground for an answer. Then she finally looks at me in my eyes and I see that same twinkle that I saw in my girl Amanda eyes about an hour ago. "Thank you," she said. "I bet you tell all the girls that."

"Now you just hurt my feelings, Trish. I thought I might've made me a new friend, cause you too beautiful for us not to be friends," I say, smiling. "I don't see anything wrong with us being friends," she says turning back to her computer and blushing. She punches in some numbers on her computer and says, "The total will be $367.54. I gave you my employee discount, by the way. Will that be cash or credit?" "Depends...how you like it?" I say and start laughing. Now we flirting. She laughs and says "It don't matter; they both get the job done." And we both start laughing for a few seconds. I can sense her getting more comfortable and familiar with me. I reach in my wallet and pull out a wad of cash and pay her. We small-talk a little till she gets everything together for me. She hands me my room keys. Room 1818. She gives me my receipt, shakes my hand and slips me her number all at the same time. "Have a good night," she says. I look at the number, give her a smile and say, "It's already a good night, thanks to you." Wink my eye at her, then five seconds later I'm gone. You gotta know when to leave and the best time to leave is when you on top...

# CHAPTER 15

I went out front and got back in the truck. I look to my right and see Amanda smiling at me, nodding her head in approval. She says, "Saint, you did that! Boy, you did that!" She's proud of me. She continues, "If you stay ready, you ain't gotta get ready. Ain't that what you like to say?"

"Yeah, somethin' like that." I park the truck and grab our bags. As we walk through the main doors, I see Trish looking at me like she expects me to be alone. Her face kinda frowns up a bit, so I whisper in Amanda's ear, "Hey bae, you see that woman at the front desk?" But I quickly caught her face before she turns to look cause I ain't want it to be that obvious.

"Yeah the one you was just flirting with. I see her, what about her?"

"Well I think she in her feelings a lil' bit because she see me in here with you. I think she thought I was by myself. But I got faith in you that you can smooth that situation out.

Can you do that for us?" I say. She says, "Of course I can, say no more." This my first time getting to see her in action, so I really don't know what to expect. This is actually a big test, because this is gonna determine how much work I gotta put in getting her ready to be the shark I need her to be in this ocean of opportunity. I watch her walk over to Trish. Amanda has her head held high. I watch as they small-talk for a little while, then they start laughing. They both look at me and nod their heads in agreement, then started laughing again. Then they went back to their conversation. I was smiling inside because I was actually proud of my girl Amanda. After about five minutes they hug and wave goodbye to each other. As Amanda starts walking back to me, I look around her to sneak a peek at Trish. We lock eyes. She starts blushing and waves goodbye, so I wave goodbye back. She did it.

# CHAPTER 16

I waited for us to get in the elevator before I looked at her and asked her, "So we must be Gucci, how ya'll was vibin' and she was waving goodbye to me just now."

"I told you I got us. We all we got." Then she pressed the 18ᵗʰ floor button on the elevator. She gave me a hug and said, "I think me and her got a lot in common."

"What you mean by that? Ya'll only talked for a few minutes."

"Well, for example, neither one of us has kids. Both of us been single for over a year. Both of us are tired of living from day to day and hustle to hustle...and...."

"And WHAT?" I said.

"And we both see sumthin' in you that we never saw in any other man we know," she said. "I told her, it's just sumthin' about you, I can't put a finger on it. You got *it* whatever the hell *it* is. And the dream and the vision that you presented me with while we was sittin' in the truck in front of my sister house just blew my mind. It's like…that's what I was already thinking without even having to say it cause you already knew how I felt and we barely even knew each other. But I felt like I've known you all my life. I felt like we was one. I automatically wanted to trust and follow you. It's like, wherever you go, I want to be there with you. Does that make sense?" She asked with a serious face.

I said, "Of course it does, baby girl." We got off the elevator on the 18th floor and, as we walked to the room, I thought for a second then said, "Damn. Ya'll talked about all that in five minutes? You good!"

We laughed all the way till we got to room 1818. I opened the door and let her go inside first so that I could see the expression on her face when she walked into the 'White House'. I call it that because everything inside is white; the curtains, carpet, sofa. Her eyes got bigger than I've ever seen before. She was definitely impressed. Then she said, beaming, "OH my God! So THIS how we livin'?" She started singing the rap song, "Ain't no mo' goin' broke, ain't no mo' goin' broke," and she started dancing and jumping on me all excited. It looked like she wanted to jump up and down on the bed, but I'm thinking the plush white comforter probably stopped her from doing it. "I LOVE it! I hope we don't ever leave!"

"This just the beginning baby girl. It's levels to this, and this just the first one. But all this comes with a price. I need you to step ya game up!"

She said, "Say no more." We chit chatted for a lil' bit, then she said, "Papi, we been on the road all day." Looking me straight in the face: "Will you take a hot shower with me?"

I thought to myself for a second. I knew that she might do something like this, and for this whole thing to work, I probably needed to put this dick on her. So, I responded like a real 'G' would, "Of course, I will". She led me by the hand into the master bathroom. She proceeded to undress me. She started with taking off my shirt, actually she ripped it in half! I ain't know she was that strong. She told me to sit on the bathroom counter so she could turn the shower on. It started getting extra hot. There was steam everywhere. I kicked off my shoes. All that she had on by now was her bra and those tight, little shorts. She walked back over to me and started kissing me on my neck, then my chest. I grabbed the back of her head...gently though. Then I told her, "Don't hold back. If you gon' fuck me, you better fuck me good, cause if another girl had the chance, she damn sure would."

She whispered, "You know I will." She kissed on my chest and worked her way down to my belt. She unhooked it with her teeth, then slowly pulled my belt out from around me. I was still sitting on the counter, looking down at her with pride because she was taking the initiative, without being told.

After she got my belt off, she took it and put it around my neck, bringing my face close to hers. She put her tongue in my mouth and our tongues wrestled slightly as she put both of her hands between my legs. I got an erection immediately. She sucks on my bottom lip, then my top lip, then steps back a little and slowly unzips my pants. She pulls my zipper down, while staring in my eyes. She pulls my pants down and throws them to the floor. I try to help her with my boxers, but she pushes my hand away, "I got this," she whispers. She pulls my boxers off and just stands there for a couple of seconds basking in the glory of what God has blessed me with. My blessing eventually becomes hers. She takes my throbbing dick in her hand and begins to slow stroke it. I pull her a little closer and unsnap her bra. I throw her bra on the bathroom floor while I run my tongue from the top of her left breast to the bottom, and then slowly around the areola. I see her perky pink nipple get extra hard. I proceed to do the same thing to her right breast and that nipple grew as long and hard as the other one. I run my tongue down the middle of her breast down to her stomach and let my tongue play around her navel. I slide off the counter and snatch her shorts, then her panties off. The steam from the hot shower is getting both of us all sweaty. I lift her up and she wraps her legs around me. I carry her into the shower, and the hot water runs over our bodies. She gets down on her knees and starts at the tip with her tongue. Her tongue slides up and down my shaft for a few minutes, then she decides to put it all in her mouth. In and out, in and out, very meticulous, precise and slow. I don't know how she knows that I love slow head, that shit feels good as fuck. She even tries to deep throat it, which is a task in itself, but she did the best she could, which was actually better than most. "Don't choke on it," I tell her. She actually has some of the best oral skills I ever experienced. She puts my testicles in her mouth and massages them with her tongue. I think to myself..*I'm all in.* I pull her up off her knees and stand her underneath the shower with one leg on the edge of the tub and bend her over doggy style. I start by licking the back of her neck, then I run my tongue down her back while massaging her clit with my middle finger. I'm using a slow, circular motion to make sure I get her fully aroused. She starts moaning, "Don't stop. Please, don't stop." And I didn't. I put that same middle finger inside of her. She starts gyrating and moving her hips in a winding motion. She's about to orgasm, but before she does, I take my right hand and put three fingers inside her mouth. Her legs are quivering and she's using the shower walls to balance herself. I take my middle finger out of her vagina and all in one motion I drop down on my knees and start to kiss her clit from the back. All the while thinking to myself, *If you gon' do it, do it right Saint.* So I did. I use my tongue to caress the walls of her insides, strumming them gently, almost like a violin player. Her legs are shaking and she's moaning God's name, "Oh my God! Oh my God!!" After ten minutes of this, she pushes me back in the tub, the shower water still running on us, and my dick is rock hard. She put her legs across mine in a straddling position, with both of her hands on my chest. She finds this dick with no help from her hands and slides down the pole as far as she can. "Good girl," I whisper in her ear. She isn't quite prepared to take the whole thing, but she takes like 75% of it. "Oh papi, Oh papi, damn this feels SO GOOD!" After six or seven strokes she starts shaking like she's having a seizure and she's scratching my chest, yelling, "I'm cumming! I'm cumming! I'm cumming!" She lays her head on my chest, trying to catch her breath from her explosion. Steam's all over the bathroom.

Now we're laying chest-to-chest and I grab her ass cheeks and spread them apart, penis still inside. Time to initiate the next round! She's biting on my neck, "Please don't stop...PLEASE!" voice raspy but still determined. I grab her by the back of her hair with my left hand, as my right hand keeps her ass cheeks spread apart. I take it into overdrive. "Where you think you goin'?" I ask when she attempts to pull back a little. Faster, harder, faster, harder. She's screaming, "Saint! Saint!" so loud that I'm 100% positive the neighbors know my name. She collapses; the water's starting to get cold now. I let her catch her breath for a few moments, then tap her on her shoulder and let her know it's time to get out.

We each grab a towel and walk into the bedroom. I can see her body still shaking just a lil' bit. It's clear who won that round. As I'm drying myself off, she's sitting on the edge of the bed, staring at me the entire time, almost embarrassed, like she had done something wrong. "Hold your head up high and straighten your face up!" I say. "You see how me and you just fucked for almost two hours?" A small smile creeps onto her face and she says, "Yeah. We did that."

"Well that was a test and you got a perfect score. Now I need you to fuck and suck these white men and women the same way, but even better. I want you to break they ass for everything they got. *They* gon' be the ones who gon' make us rich. *We* gone be rich baby girl. All from what we just did in that bathroom. You good at what you do, and it's my job to make you great." She shook her head and silently agreed. I think she understood that would be our last time ever having sex; it's strictly business from now on. "I understand papi."

"But, I'm gonna need you to multi-task. It ain't gon' be all about sex. We gon' be doing a lil' bit of everything. I just need you to be patient. Patience is a virtue. We gonna pick up about 4-6 more girls along the way, and YOU gon' be the one to get the girls for us."

She got it. "Anything you need me to do papi. Say no more. The first day we met, you told me you had a master plan. I love that I get to be a part of it." I kiss her on the forehead. "Get some rest. Showtime tomorrow." She finishes drying off, then lies down under the blanket and dozes off.

I throw on some gym shorts, grab my headphones out my bag and grab my phone. I go through my music list and find me some Jeezy - Thug Motivation 101. I let it play from #1 till the end, then put it on repeat. I'm sitting on the edge of the bed planning my next five steps. Life is chess, not checkers. I'm up all night planning. This ain't the time to sleep. The only thing that comes to sleepers is dreams. So long ago, I started hating sleep. I took a 30-minute cat nap. As the sun rose up, I rose up with it. Time to go to work!

# CHAPTER 17

8:45am…

I get dressed and put the TV on the local news station while I wait for room service to bring the breakfast I ordered, and my newspaper. Fifteen minutes later it arrives; grits, eggs, sausage, bacon, toast and biscuits. But for me I ordered a whole grain bagel, a large orange juice and cream cheese with a granola bar on the side. Brain food. I give the room service a tip and go to wake up Amanda. "Rise and grind baby girl."

She wakes up smiling. She yawns and says, "Good morning. I haven't slept that good in years." She looks around the room and sees the breakfast on the table. "Is that for me? I hope so because I'm starving!" She gets out of the bed, walks over to the table and sits down. "Of course it is", I say. I'm seated at the table as well; the only difference is that I have the business section of the newspaper in my hand. I'm focused. "Thanks. So what's the plan for today?"

she asked, "I know tonight I start work at The Premiere, but I'm talking about in-between time."

"First you gon' eat. Then you gon' get dressed. Then we gon' hit the mall to get you something to wear to work. While you were sleeping, I used that time to regroup. What I came up with, was that we gon' post your picture on Backpage, CityVibe, Seeking Arrangement and Sugardaddy.com, and set you up some dates. We really looking for white males, young and old. We looking for people that we can trust a little bit. Even though I'll be there with you the whole step of the way." She finishes eating then gets up to get dressed, while I finish reading the paper; trying to keep up with current events.

We catch the elevator downstairs to the main floor. Before we get to the lobby I whisper to her, "Go ask Trish if she wants to hang out with us for a while." It was about five minutes till she got off work; this was a good way for me to see where her head was at. She said, "OK." I waved to Trish as I walked through the lobby on my way to get the truck. Really, I needed them couple of minutes alone to strategize. I got to the truck, crunk it up and sit in there for a second. That's when it hits me; let them go shopping together, let them vibe a little bit. I put the truck in reverse and drive to the front entrance. Before I get out the truck, I leave $500 in the armrest. I hop out, go to the lobby and I see them walking through the lobby together, laughing and hugging.

Amanda says, "You ready papi?" I say, "Yeah, I'm ready, but there's been a change of plans. I want you two to go together. I'm gon' stay here and map some things out." They both look at each other and say at the same time, "Alright!" I give them each a hug. I hand Amanda the keys and tell her that I left $500 in the armrest and to be safe. They wave goodbye and drive off. *Planting seeds...*

# CHAPTER 18

While the girls are shopping, I stay in the room, plotting. First, I need Amanda to close that deal with Trish, which I know she can and will. When that little situation is set, that'll be two females I'll have on my way to my starting five. Both are beautiful and useful in their own way. Amanda's very outgoing and she's good at reading people's body language and facial expressions. Plus, she knows how to make a man feel like a man; special. Trish...now her personality is the exact opposite of Amanda's. Trish is a lil' shy and not as straight forward, but I can tell that she'll open up very quickly if she feels comfortable with you. That's where I come in; where my two ladies come up short. I give them what they lack. They seem to like each other, and are getting along quite well. All they lack in life is a dude like me, and now they got me! If I can get these two on the same page, my book will have a nice beginning. I'm gon' do it a lil' different with Trish. Me and her ain't gon' have sex at all. It's gonna be a straight mental relationship with her, as long as Amanda keeps her mouth shut about what we did together sexually, which I'm sure she will, but, we'll see.

Since I got the room to myself for a couple of hours, I take out my iPad and go through the playlist. Poison Clan - Poisonous Mentality. I have to get back to my roots. I don't mind girls catching feelings for me, in fact, I *need* them to have feelings for me, but they have to be directed at the right place. Not necessarily the heart, but more of the mind, cause that's where our connection starts and that's what'll keep us together. So, Step #1: I wanna put them both in the gentleman's club just to get this cash to start flowin'. We'll do that for a couple of days or a couple of weeks, it depends on how things are going. Step #2: We're heading out west. First stop, Houston for a lil' while, but that's just a pit stop on our way to Vegas. *"Go big or go home"*, ain't that what they say? *"What happens in Vegas, stays in Vegas."* Step #3: My cash should be up a lil' bit by then, so I wanna take the girls out the strip club and go cyber; full time; Backpage and CityVibe to start. Step #4: Pick me up three more girls, either in Atlanta or Houston, but I want five to make my team complete. I want one of each race cause I like 'em "brown, yellow, Puerto Rican and Haitian!"

Now, when the girls get back, I'm not gonna flood 'em with all this information at one time. First I need to see if Trish is onboard. Plus, they don't need to know *everything* right this second. Only what I tell 'em! I think I just mapped out the steps to achieving an empire. 'Ain't no mo' goin' broke', keeps playing in my head.

Now let me rest my eyes for a few till they get back from the store.

# CHAPTER 19

I'm laying down on the couch when I hear the hotel room door open and my ladies walk in.

"Hey papi."

"Hey Saint."

Then they put their bags on the bed.

"Hey na! How'd the shopping go?"

Trish replies first, "It went well. We had a good conversation. Sounds interesting. You wanna tell me more?"

"I sure do. Let's all have a seat at the table."

We all sit down around the table and they both look at me like students enthralled by their teacher.

I start with saying, "First off, Trish, I'm glad you're interested in what we got goin' on. I don't know what all Amanda told you, but I trust her and I know she knows how to hold her own." She nods her head in agreement, as did Amanda. "Second off, we would be happy to have you. I know you'd be a great asset to the team. We want you and we need you." She starts smiling. "Since you been with Amanda all day, I know she told you that we do whatever we gotta do to get that dough. We gonna be at the top and we want you with us. I like your vibe and the glow you give off." Trish starts blushing, then says "I told Amanda the same thing about you."

I smile. "Great minds think alike. So what I need ya'll to do is let me lead and I need ya'll to follow, without question. Cause if we gon' make it to the top, it's gon' be my brains and ya'll beauty that take us there, ya dig?"

Trish says, "I'm flattered. And…and, it really does all seem very intriguing. But I'm just a small town girl from Kentucky. I don't think I'm really cut out for this type of thing." OK. So she's not fully there yet. But she wants to be convinced, I can tell. She wouldn't be here right now if she didn't. Time to pull back a little.

"Ok. I understand. So, what's your story, Trish? What did you do before you started working here? Where do you see yourself in five years?" I asked her almost the exact same questions I asked Amanda, but in a different way and a different tone.

"Well, like I said, I'm originally from Lexington, Kentucky...born and raised. I been here in Atlanta for about seven months. I don't have any kids, maybe later on in life, but now's not the time. I'm 23 years old. My parents are from Guyana, but they both died in a car crash when I was 9, and I kinda just bounced around from family member to family member after that. I'm single, well, for now anyway...." She paused for a second, looked up at me, almost embarrassed, but went on. "I admit, I was instantly attracted to you and if I had the guts, I wouldn't even mind being a part of the team, but... I'm just not that outgoing and it sucks because I'm not happy with this job and where I'm at in life right now. They pay me minimum wage and the boss treats me like shit. In five years, I just wanna live the good life and see the world. Ya' know? But I honestly don't know how I'm gonna get there." She looks me straight in my eyes, waiting for an answer.

I say, "Let me ask you this? Can you quit your job right now if I need you to?"

She doesn't answer right away, just looks off at the ceiling like it's a life or death question. Finally, she answers "I don't know about quitting my job and all that. I mean, I like ya'll, I think ya'll are cool, but that's a huge step for me. I'm just not that...impulsive." She looks down at the ground like she said something wrong. But she was right. This was a big decision for her to make, with two people she just met. I understand completely. But, I don't give up that easily. I take my right index finger and put it under her chin and lift her head up so that we were eye to eye. "Do you know what a job is?" I know that she *thought* she knew, but I want to give her *my* version. I think I may have offended her, because of the tone in her voice when she answered, "Yeah I know what a job is! That's what I was doing when you met me...MY JOB!" I got her tough ass now. I tell her, "Yeah, you right. But a job, a j-o-b, is 'just over broke'. Now, I know you said you was making just above minimum wage. That ain't shit baby girl. How about you do this for me? As a matter of fact, do this for *us*; just hang out with us and see how you like our lifestyle. I guarantee, you'll never go back to your j-o-b again!" I can tell she's thinking hard. Finally, she says, "I can do that. There's nothing wrong with hanging out with two cool, new friends!" I nod my head in agreement, then say, "Just do me a favor? Keep an open mind tonight."

"Of course I will. Listen, I may look like an angel, but I got a lil' naughty side, too!"

I already knew that. But I just say, "We'll see..."

"Fair enough," she says.

Then I turn to Amanda, "Now, lemme see what you got from the store. Time for a show!"

# CHAPTER 20

I get out my wireless bluetooth speaker from my bag and connect my ipad; then go through my playlist and find something suitable for a gentleman's club. Now, there's a difference between a strip club and a gentleman's club. A gentleman's club is more upscale and the girls never get fully nude. The women wear thongs and there is hardly ever touching, and never any sex in the club. It just doesn't happen. The dress code is strictly enforced for the men and the ladies. They cater to the working, business class. Gang members and attire are not allowed, so there is rarely an issue of violence. A strip club is different. For the most part, the women get completely naked and have to do much more to make a buck. Some of them resort to tricks, such as shoving beer bottles deep inside them and squirting it all back out like a waterfall. There's even backroom sex involved a lot of the times, and lap dances combined with hand jobs. Almost nothing is off limits, and that is *not* the type of environment I want for my girls. And I explain all of this to them both, before I start the music. I find the perfect song - Juicy J - *Bands will make her dance*. I press play and turn the speaker volume to the max. Amanda is dressed and ready to perform! She has on a red G-string with a red sequined bikini top to match; a long, sexy red see-through negligee on top of it all. She has on six-inch-high stilettos to set everything off. I like it. It compliments all of her best qualities.

I tell her to use the post of the bed as a stripper pole. Mental note: *buy a portable pole*. I tell her to make love to the pole, this is a marathon, not a sprint. Pace yourself. Ride that pole like she was riding a dick. I let her know that 80% of what she is doing is in her face. I need to see tongue action and hips rotating. Trish is sitting in the chair next to me laughing and cheering her on. If I'm not mistaken, at one point, she even looks a little aroused. I pull some money out my pocket and give Trish about $500. I tell her to make Amanda feel special. She takes it from me and starts showering her with money. Sticking bills in her shoe, her top...everywhere!

I have Amanda practice her lap dance on me, for obvious reasons. Without giving good lap dances, we might as well get out the game. But she ain't need very much help, just a lil' coaching. I tell her no kissing, and always make eye contact. The eyes are what reels the men in. Make the client feel like he's the only man in the world.

I also let her know I'll be at every show, every night. I see Trish out the corner of my eye, taking it all in. I motion for Amanda to go give her a lap dance too. Trish was loose by now and enjoying every minute. She even switched positions with Amanda and started dancing on her. Ha! They say all women secretly wanna be a stripper for a day. It was clear that she would soon be a part of our little team. The song ended and Amanda skipped off to the bathroom to freshen up. Trish was still smiling and excited. "I never had a lap dance before. That was pretty awesome," she said, eyes beaming.

Amanda comes back in the room a few minutes later with just her robe on and lies across the bed.

"Good job baby girl. Now, you gonna have guys come at you all types of ways, which is cool, but what this conversation is about is *price*. If they talkin' about sex, they better be talkin' about $1000 or better, cause you top of the line. And if they talking about oral sex, they betta be talkin' $500 or better. They won't ever be able to say you were cheap. Got it?"

"Yeah, I got it," Amanda said.

I got up and started picking up all of the money from off the floor and putting it on the table. I also took whatever I had left in my wallet, and put it on there as well. I had their full attention and I needed to put on a good show. At the end of the day, it was all about the money, and I needed them to know this. "A regular 9-5 ain't gonna get you this," I tell them, looking straight at Trish. She nodded her head in agreement.

"And another thing, these men are just customers. I know how ya'll women are, but leave those feelings at the do' and pull your panties to the side! It's all business. Ain't no love there. Ain't no feelings there. All ya' emotions are for me and vice versa. Don't get attached to any one of these customers. That's why we going for businessmen and older, married white men who don't want anything more than to have some fun, get a nut, spend a lot of money then go home to they wife. Got it?"

"Got it!"

"Now, I'm gon' promise you this; I ain't gonna let nothing happen to you...*ever*. I'm gon' keep you safe; that's my job. If you down and hurtin', *I'm* down and hurtin' and I ain't gonna let that happen. I want us to be one. I *need* us to be one. Alright?" She bobbed her head in agreement. I could tell Trish was soaking it all in. Reality is, I was talking to her just as much as I was talking to Amanda. I don't have her yet, but she's coming along slowly and surely. "Now, ya'll get some rest, chill out a bit and collect your thoughts. We got a long night ahead of us." I clicked off the speaker, plugged in my headphones and started living in my own head...

# CHAPTER 21

**7:00pm.** It's time to get ready to go to work. I wake up the girls. It's a good thing Trish is off tonight and able to hang out with us. I need her to see everything firsthand. They shower, put on that sweet-smelling lotion and body spray that women wear, and Amanda packs her bag for work. We head downstairs to the truck and get on our way!

The gentleman's club, Premiere, was at least an hour away. We already went over everything we had to go over; this ride to the club was all about setting the mood. Since we was in Atlanta, I play some Rich Homie Quan. I get my girls all crunk before we got there. I need to make sure that Trish has a good time and that Amanda is hyped enough to make a lot of money. I let them two walk in about twenty minutes before me, to grab some attention without me as a distraction. Then I walk in and go straight to the bar where Trish is sitting playing video games, and order a Hennessy straight on the rocks, and a Long Island for her, to loosen her up a little. I chill at the bar for a l'il while before I head to the stage. Me personally, I ain't tipping no woman but my own for a dance, unless I'm try'na get that woman to come and work for me.

I get to the stage and see Amanda up there by herself. She does everything I asked her to do. Man, she is doing so damn good, it seems only right for me to go in my pocket and break her off. So, I do! I tip her 'bout two hundred dollars full of ones and fives. I am so impressed, that I grab Trish from the bar and ask her to sit at the stage and tip her too. I give her about three hundred dollar bills, just to start out. We make Amanda the center of attraction for the night. There are some fine ladies in there, but I shine the spotlight on *mine*. I throw money from the ceiling. Money is pouring down from everywhere! I love it and so did they. I must be doin' a good job making it rain, because it challenges a few of the other men to come and try to outdo me. Before I know it, the stage is stacked at least two feet high full of money, and Amanda doesn't even seem to notice. She is in the moment! "Always business, never personal," I whisper in her ear. She smiles and begins to take advantage of the moment. She gives every dude who was in front of that stage at least a minute of personal attention. The goal is to lock 'em in, then break the bank!

When her set is finished she collects all of her money, gets off the stage and goes in the back to count it, and change. I tell Trish to stay by the stage and keep tipping the ladies. I tell her to watch how they move. Watch how they look at people. Make mental notes of what makes the men dig in their pockets.

In the meantime, I float around the club, just try'na see what I can see. That's when I spot her, another girl that belongs on my team, she just don't know it yet. I have to approach her in a straight-forward way. "Hey beautiful, now you *know* you need to be fuckin' with me. What you waitin' for?" I had my lil' sly grin on. She looks upset because she apparently hadn't made any money.

"You wanna dance or what?" she said, looking all serious.

"Do I want a dance? No. I want more than a dance." She was waiting for me to finish the rest of my sentence. "I want your heart. I want your loyalty. Your dedication. I wanna keep a smile on your face, cause you don't look very happy right now." She looks down for a few seconds, then looks me in my face and says, "Damn! You want a whole lot from me! But you right, I ain't happy. How *you* gon' make me smile, cause I sure need it!"

"It's a million and one ways for me to get and keep a smile on your face. Where you want me to start?"

"Start from the beginning," she says.

Okay, I got her full attention now. "First, I'll take you out of here and bring you with me. Second, I'll introduce you to a life you never imagined. Third, I'm on my way to the moon and I want you to come with me. Fourth, I see better things for you than you see for yourself. I need you...." She put up her hand as if to say "Hold up, I heard enough."

"OK, OK, I hear you. All of that sounds good, but, where do we go from *here*?"

"Where you wanna go?" I ask.

"Depends. Where you wanna take me?" I smirk a l'il. "Everywhere. You ready?" She asked for my phone and put her number in it. "Call me when you think I'm ready. And by the way, what's your name? What they call you?" She hands back my phone. "They call me Saint, and I'll call you when the time is right." I walk away to go find Trish. She is still at the stage, tipping and having a good ole' time. I buy her another drink; then tell her I'll be right back. I walk out the club and to my truck to gather my thoughts. *Job well done*, I tell myself....

# CHAPTER 22

Amanda put in another hour or so at the club. She was dancing with customers when I walked back in. I gave her a nod of approval, to let her know that she was doing a good job, then I tapped my watch to let her know that it was almost time to go. Trish almost looked sad.

It was 4:20am when she finally got done. Me and Trish were already outside in the truck waiting, when she walked out. Amanda got in the front and Trish sat directly behind her in the backseat. I turn to face Amanda, "Good job baby girl, I'm proud of you." Trish is smiling ear to ear, hugging her from behind and said, "You did good girl! It didn't look as hard as I thought it would be. And it looked *fun*!"

"It was an adrenaline rush," Amanda said. "When you two came to the stage and threw all that money on me, and then everybody else started throwing money too...OH MY GOD!!! My pussy started throbbing!!" They both start laughing. Then she goes in her purse and pulls out three huge wads of cash. Following her lead, I pull out all the other cash I have in my pockets and put everything in clear view for both girls to see what comes from hard work. It looks like a million dollars, in *their* eyes anyway. Really, it's maybe just three or four grand, but I see their eyes and I know they never seen this kind of money before. At least not at one time. I have to play it cool, like this was just a typical day in the life. And it will be, if they just listen to me. I think it's now time for a l'il speech. I look at both of them and say, "This gon' happen for us every night if ya'll listen to me and if ya'll trust me. I promise, I won't lead you wrong." I have my sincere face on. And I really was. "This just the beginning. We gon' take the world by storm. Buy us a couple houses, some nice cars, start a few businesses. We gon' get rich, I promise you." I look directly at Amanda first, "Baby girl, you wit' me?" I already know the answer; I just need her to say it in front of Trish. "Duh papi, you know I'm wit' you. What kind of question is that?" I just smile at her. "That's what I like to hear." Now, the tough part…trying to get Trish onboard. Amanda knows it too because we both turn and look at her at the same time. I say, "We just showed you a little bit of how we roll. Now my question to you, is you wit' us?" She pauses for a few seconds. Then she nods her head real slow; the words finally come out and she says, "Why the hell not? Count me in! Team US dammit!" Me and Amanda both high-five her. "Welcome to the team boo!" Amanda says. While the girls are still laughing and smiling, I put the truck in Drive and we take off. In more ways than one! Shit, with all of this going on, I almost forget about the new girl I met tonight. Things are starting to look up!

My motto is...you can catch more bees with honey than with vinegar, which translates to me not ever disrespecting my girls...*ever*! Nobody else will disrespect my girls, either. I'll make sure that they have all they want and need, while they with me; that's my job. I ain't worried about no other woman or man taking them from me. That's how confident you have to be in this industry. I rather be loved than feared...that's just me though.

I put the money in the armrest, *I'll count it later*, I think to myself. Then I ask the girls, "Ya'll hungry?" I know they probably are, because I sure am.

"Yeah, I can eat sumthin', how 'bout you Trish?" Amanda said.

"Most definitely! Where we going this time of the morning? Oh, wait! Let's go by that 24-hour Waffle House by the hotel."

"You got it!" But before I pull off, I tell the girls that I need to make a phone call right quick. I turn down the radio, go through my phone and find the newest contact that was saved in there. I hit the talk button.

# CHAPTER 23

## Part Three: TAKIN' CARE OF BUSINESS

Ring ring ring...

I say, "Can I speak to Starr?"

"Who this?"

"This Saint. You busy?"

She pauses for a few seconds, then, "Ohhh Saint! You said you was gonna call me when the time was right. So, the time must already be right, I suppose?"

"You sound like you're in better spirits. It might be the right time, I'on know yet. You still in the club?"

"Yeah, I feel a l'il better. I made a lil' money after you left, but it was that new girl who made all the money. But yeah, I'm still inside waiting for my ride to get off work so she can come pick me up. Why? Wassup?"

"I want to know if you hungry and want to grab a bite to eat with us? I'll take you home when we finish."

"Yeah, I'm starving! But, who is *us*?" she asks, sounding surprised. I say, "Me and my two lady friends. They cool. You might like 'em if you get to know 'em."

Silence. Then, "Sure. Why not, sounds like fun. Let me call my friend and let her know I got a ride. Where you at? Out front?"

"Yeah. Just walk outside and you'll see me. I'm in an all-black Cadillac Escalade with tinted windows." I hang up the phone and pull up to the front. The girls looking at me like, "Damn. You got another girl already!?" If you stay ready, you ain't gotta get ready!

"Is it that girl, Starr, the tall black girl who you was talking to tonight? I'm not being nosy or questioning you, I was just wondering cause she was kinda sexy, papi!" I laughed and said, "Yeah, that's her. She gon' be joining us for breakfast. Are you two alright with that?"

"I am," Trish said.

Amanda licked her lips and said, "I'm definitely ok with her joining us...for breakfast." Then she laughed. That's when I looked at Trish and said, "Bae? I want you to make her feel comfortable with the three of us, alright?" I looked her in the eyes. "You think you can handle that?"

She seemed to like the challenge, "Alright. I got this. I learned from the best. Just sit back and watch!" Ten minutes later, she came to the truck. I roll the window down and tell her to hop in!

# CHAPTER 24

Starr gets in the truck and everybody makes their introductions. GPS shows the Waffle House is 35 minutes away. I'm feelin' really good cause I hear and see that her and Trish are getting along very, very well. I can't really hear what they're talking about, but maybe I ain't supposed to! All I know is that I hear laughing, and me and Amanda have our own conversation going on in the front seat anyway. We get to the Waffle House and I tell the three girls to go in, get us a table and order the food. I tell them what I want and that I'd be in there in about five minutes.

After they go inside, I turn the music down so I can focus. I use those few minutes to meditate and give thanks for my blessings, cause no matter what I do in this world, I'm still blessed and thankful to be alive. Any day above ground is a blessing. After meditating, I go in the armrest, take out the money and start counting it. $700, $800...$1700...$2200...$2600! $2600! That's what she made on her very first night, which was REALLY good! I take out a hundred dollars, put it in my pocket and go inside.

"So, what'd I miss?"

"Nothin'. Just a lil' girls' talk," Starr says, smiling.

After about an hour of eating and small talk, I ask Starr a direct question. "Can you be trusted?"

"Of course I can. But trusted to do what?"

"To do whatever needs to be done," I say. "Do you wanna live like the rich folks? Drive a nice car and live in a big house? To achieve that dream, I'm gon' need you to trust me. Can you do that? Cause ain't no "I" in team, and that's what I'm forming, and those two girls right there...," I say, pointing to Trish and Amanda, "...are my stars, but I'm lookin' for possibly three more. We have a mutual love and respect for each other, that's why this works so good for us. Understand?"

"I understand. And I saw first-hand how your 'star' did tonight. I definitely don't mind being a part of THAT! I'm game!"

"Hold on. Slow down. Listen...me and those two girls don't have any problems at all. We don't argue, we don't fight. They don't talk back because they know I'll never tell them nothing wrong. They don't question my intentions, cause my intentions are genuine. They trust me fully and I trust them fully. What's theirs is mine and what's mine is theirs. That's love! Are you on that? Cause I got zero tolerance for foolishness and I'm not gon' let no bad apple ruin my tree. You feel that?"

She says, "Look...I've never been a part of anything in my life. I'm used to doing shit on my own. But what I always *have* been, is loyal to those who are loyal to me. I ain't never been no 'bad seed'. I'm more of a sweet peach. I'm a good girl. I'll fit right in, you ain't gonna have no problems out of me. I promise. I'm on that."

I look at her for a few seconds. "OK. I'll give you a shot. I figure the girls told you a lil' bit about how we roll, right?"

"Yeah, they told me. Put me on a probation period." There goes that familiar twinkle again.

"Alright, Miss Starr. You got it. I'll be in touch with you real soon."

We finish up our breakfast, I pay the bill and we leave the diner. She gives me her address, I put it in the GPS, and we ride out. She is about fifteen minutes away. We get to her place and I tell her I'll be calling her again soon. I wait till she gets safely inside her door and wave goodbye. Before I pull off, I give both my girls a kiss and say, "Good job ladies". Off to the room we go...

# CHAPTER 25

Three weeks later…

I wake up that morning around 10am. We start packing up the room because it's about time for us to relocate. We been here too long; it's time to shift. Trish transitioned beautifully into her role on the team. She was a natural performer. Her and Amanda were a perfect team. Every night was a good night for them, and I didn't want them to wear out their welcome.

I leave the girls in the room to finish packing up as I excuse myself. I go out on the balcony and close the door behind me. I'd been gone several weeks now, so it was time to check in with my kids. I call Lashonda first. Ring ring ring…

"Hello?"

"Hey wassup? How you doin'?"

"I'm good Saint, How about you?"

"I'm coolin'. How's my son doin?"

"He's doing fine. He's at my mama house right now. What's going on?"

"Not much. I just wanted to tell him I love him. Check this out; I'm going to the bank this morning to start a bank account for him. Anything you need, get it out that account. I'm gonna overnight you the ATM card and the pin when I get it, alright?"

"Thanks! We need it. He starts school soon and I was try'na get him some new clothes and some shoes this weekend."

"No need to thank me, that's my child." Then another thought comes to mind, "Ay, can you do me a favor, since you going school shopping this weekend?"

She was silent. Then, "Depends on what it is."

"I would like you and Talia to take the kids shopping together. I want both of my kids to spend as much time together as possible. I'm out of town right now, but I'll be back in a few weeks. The same thing I'm tellin' you, when we hang up, I'm gon' call Talia and tell her too. So, can you do that for me?"

"No problem."

"Cool. And another thing, I want ya'll to take the kids to Chuck E Cheese, and whatever else they want. I'm putting $1000 in each of ya'll account, ok?"

"Of course that's ok. And yeah, we gonna take these kids to do something fun." She paused, then said, "Baby daddy?"

"Wassup ma?"

"Whatever you out there doing...be safe, alright?"

I said, "I will."

That went smoother than I thought it would! One down, one to go....

# CHAPTER 26

Now, it was time for me to call Talia. She was the easy one to deal with. She was funny, sexy, smart and supportive. All she really wants is for me to succeed and do good in life so that I can be a good role model for our son.

Ring ring ring…

"Hey Papi."

"Hey ma. What's good wit' it?"

"Nothin'. On my way to work. Long time, no hear from!"

I felt kinda bad taking so long to reach out. "I know. I been out of town try'na get straight. You know me, I want my kids wit' the finest of everything…and that takes money! So, I'm on my grind, right now."

"You right, I *do* know you, that's why I hope you staying out of trouble. You know Zion needs you. You just got in his life, we don't want you taken away for another three years…or worse. *We* need you."

"I know; I'm just up here making a couple of moves real quick. Don't nothin' come to sleepers but dreams, mama!"

She chuckled a little bit, "You always got an answer for everything!"

"I know, right," I laughed too. "But check this out Talia. I got a quick question for you. You still got a bank account, right? And DON'T WORRY, this ain't for nothin' illegal."

"Yeah. I do. Wassup?"

"Well, I made a couple of dollars while I been here, so I'm gon' put about $1000 cash in your account so you can take my son school shopping, if that's OK?"

She paused, then softly said, "Yeah, that's OK. I'm proud of you Saint."

"Thanks. But I got one condition…my other son, King, and his mom are going school shopping this weekend as well, and I want all four of ya'll to go together. I want my sons to bond and I want you two to have a good relationship for the kids cause I love all four of ya'll. Can you do that for me?"

She didn't even hesitate, "Yes, I can. As long as you keep handling your biz, anything for you!"

PERFECT! "OK, cool. I'm gon' give you her number so ya'll can make the arrangements. Text me your account info and the money will be in there by the morning."

*Handled.*

Now, from the outside looking in, people might think, 'damn, that was easy', but this was a work in progress. If anyone thinks that I just woke up one day and they magically became friends, they'd be wrong.

See, I been dealing with Talia since 8th grade. For over ten years, we been on and off. That's why I was so surprised that she continued to deal with me when we both went off to Bethune-Cookman, and she found out about Lashonda. Now, Lashonda knew that I was in a relationship, but it was one of those things that kinda just happened. I flirted. She flirted. We flirted. Eventually Talia found out, because I got sloppy, and she kicked me out, so…off to Shonda I went. Her and Shonda fought every chance they got. When one of 'em would get mad and kick me out, I'd go right to the other one. This went on for several years, so I figured we just had an understanding; I loved them both. I was their man and they were my girls. We never had a problem with another man and they never had a problem with another woman. What we had took time to develop, with me paying the cost to be the boss. My granddad once told me, "A man could have fifteen girlfriends as long as he could afford to take care of all fifteen." And that made sense to me, even at a young age. And I wasn't greedy, I didn't even want fifteen. I only wanted two.

Anyway…I ain't trying to make them into best friends. I just want my sons to be raised as brothers, not half-brothers, and they understand that. They both agreed that if I handled my business, they would handle theirs. And of course, I always handle my business…

# CHAPTER 27

Now I got the wheels in motion for things to move how I need them to move even when I'm not around. I got my kid's mothers communicating. I need them to connect on another level for us. I ain't want no animosity, no jealousy, no hating, no lies and no secrets between the three of us. We have to show a united foundation for the kids. I don't know if me and either one of them will ever be together again, but we will always be bonded through my boys.

I open the balcony door and go back into the room. The girls packed everything up and we're ready to ride! While we're on the elevator, I tell them I have to make a quick pit stop at the bank. I try to keep them in the loop on almost everything. Trish is just so excited to be traveling, she can't wait to ask, "So, Saint baby, where we going next?"

"I don't know yet. I'm just gon' drive west, then ya'll can pick the spot. Alright?"

So, we're headed west, music on shuffle, gettin' our l'il vibe on. I'm so tired from the night before, that I didn't get to ask them how they felt about Starr and what they thought of her officially joining the team. She hung out with us a few times since that first night we all met, but before I brought her on I wanted to make sure the other two perfected their game. I think now would be a good time. I turn down the music and get semi-serious with them, "So, let me ask you guys somethin'." They were both focused on me. "What do ya'll think of Starr? Do ya'll get along with her? You think she's ready to join the team now?" They both kind of speak at the same time; "She cool."

"We like her. I mean, she came off kind of rough at first cause she ain't know us and she was probably jealous cause we was making all the money," Amanda said. "But she cool with us now. We can use her."

I tell them, "That's understandable, but once she got to know ya'll, she softened up. I actually like her *because* of how tough she is. I believe I can send her out with you guys and if a female or dude get out of control, or out of hand in any kind of way, she gon' curse they ass out! Yeah…she's definitely a lil' rough around the edges. But we can use that to our advantage."

See, all three girls bring something different to the table. Starr has that street edge that the other two lacked. For all I know, she might even carry a razor blade under her tongue!

But she was soft on me, and that's all that really mattered. I think I'll give her a try when we get to the new location. I ain't gon' tell them about it yet, though, I'm gonna surprise them with it.

We drive for about 35 minutes and Trish spots this one hotel in Decatur. It actually looks pretty good...The Clevelander. I pull up to the front and got out to check in. This time around, I get a room with two king sized beds. I want everyone to feel comfortable. We ride to the 15th floor and proceed to room 1505, penthouse suite. The hotel is nice on the outside and in the hallways, but when I open the room door. *Oh, Shit!* This is better than the 'W'! Everything in the room is royal purple. When the girls walk in, they say the same thing I did..."Oh SHIT!", but they say it at the same time, and out loud. They drop their bags and go and lie across the beds. In my mind, I know this was just the beginning.

I tell Trish, "Good job bae. You picked a nice spot. We gon' be here for a few days before we head out of Georgia." They both smile and started unpacking. I tell them to settle in and order a pizza or something; I'd be back shortly. I have a few things to handle. On the elevator down to my truck, I call our newest family member, Starr.

Ring ring ring…

"Hello," she answered.

"Hey boo. What you doin'?"

"Just got my hair done. What *you* doin'?"

"Shiddd...I'm on my way to come get you. You ready?"

"I'm ready, but where we going? I'm only askin' cause I need to know how to dress."

"You comin' wit' me, wherever I go. I want you to pack up all your stuff. It's showtime!"

She didn't even think about it, "It's about time. You on your way now?"

"Yeah. I'll be there in about an hour. Be ready."

"Alright I will." Click. That was easy.

Now, time to surprise the girls. I was on the brink of building my team, and they were all diverse and unique in how they look and act.

I'm on my way...

# CHAPTER 28

Starr got in the truck with what she called her 'whole life', three duffle bags. It was time for a change for her, and *I* was that change. As she got in the truck, this was my first time really noticing how sexy she was. She was damn near 6ft tall, long black hair, slim waist and a nice l'il ass. She's actually VERY beautiful. Guess I've never really seen her in the daylight. I liked everything about her, including her attitude. She had that foreign look. Like you'd expect her to speak with an accent when she opened her mouth. I ask where she's from and she tells me the Dominican Republic, but she was raised in North Carolina. She got those light brown eyes that are hard to get mad at.

I know the girls have given her the rundown on how I do business, but I feel like it's my responsibility to tell her myself so she can hear it straight outta the horse's mouth. I kinda broke her down a little bit, but not to where I need her to be. She says she's not a bad seed, but I can already see me having to check her a couple of times. And really...I ain't try'na break her, I'm try'na *build* her. From the outside looking in, it would seem like one man's trash is another man's treasure. But I don't think Starr was ever anyone's trash; she definitely may have been their headache, though!

"Starr, this is a team and I'm the coach, the owner, the assistant coach, the president, the vice president and the CEO! I ain't arguing with nobody about NOTHING, I don't have the time or the desire. I say that to say, anything my girls need, I supply. My dreams are their dreams. We all wanna be successful. All the money the girls make, comes to me. I make all the decisions. They trust me and I haven't let them down yet, you get it?"

She let all of the information that she just heard from me settle in, then she spoke after a few moments, "I hear you, loud and clear. I respect that you're making sure we have a clear understanding before we really get started, but the girls already told me all of that. But it sounds better coming from you. And all that what you said, I agree and I don't have a problem with any of it, so count me in, don't count me out." She starts digging in her purse, "All I made was about $550 last night. I spent $100 on my hair and got some food so I have about $350 left, after I give my roommate $100 towards rent, but it's yours." This was a good start for her just coming in. Her money will get better once I put her around the other girls', full time. I smile and say "OK, then it's official. The girls gon' be surprised and glad to see you. They don't know you coming. We just moved to a new spot this morning and you gon' love it! Oh yeah, another thing, none of my girls do drugs. That's a problem that I ain't dealing with, cool?"

"Cool," she says as we pull up to the hotel. I don't want to have *any* misunderstandings. Even though I like Starr as a person, there's just somethin' about her that I can't put my finger on. It's like I can read her 95% of the time…but it's that 5% that I'm concerned about. *Shit,* but I ain't concerned enough to not let her work with me. I am definitely gonna keep my eye on her, though. And my other two girls will be my eyes and ears when I ain't around, since they'll be spending a lot of time with her.

# CHAPTER 29

I get her three bags out the back of the truck and we go through the lobby to the elevator, up to the 15th floor. When we get to the room, I tell her to stand on the side of the wall by the door so that the girls wouldn't see her. I take the key card out and open the door and walk in. Both of the girls look at me, the TV's on and the shower's running. They're both in their panties and bras. "I'm back and I brought ya'll a surprise!" They stop what they're doing and they both look at me…waiting. "What is it papi?"

"Surprise!! Did you miss me?" Starr said as she ran up to the girls. They start hugging each other, smiling from ear to ear. They seem really glad to see each other. I grab Starr's bags from out the hallway and put them in the closet. I let the girls get comfortable, as far as the showers and everything else they need to do. I figure it'd be a good time to go to the bank and put that money in the account for the kids before I start my day. I tell them I'll be right back.

I check my text messages to retrieve the account info for Talia, I already saved Lashonda's. I slide to the bank real quick to handle my biz. I put $1000 in each of their accounts like I said I would because I'm a man of my word. I make another quick stop to pick up something special for my three girls.

I'm headed back to the hotel, but decide to check out the strip club in the area. It's upscale-looking from the outside, but it's the inside that got me. Club Secrets is hooked up! It has six stages, with spotlights on each one, and three separate bars. I could see my girls making a million dollars in this place, so I decide to talk to the manager, on a manager's level. If he couldn't tell me what I needed to hear, I'd talk to the owner next. But for now, the manager will do. I walk directly up to him and ask if we can go somewhere and talk for a minute. He agrees, so we get a corner table and ordered two Hennys, straight. I ask his name. Larry Weinstein...it figures. "Mr. Weinstein, I'm a businessman and businessmen talk business." He nodded his head, "You're right. So I guess this is a business meeting! What's on your mind, Sir? By the way, what shall I call you?"

"They call me Saint, and what's on my mind, is that I wanna bring some fresh, new money into your establishment."

"And what do you mean new money, cause all money ain't good money for this kind of business," he said.

"You're right about that. But this new money that I'm talkin' about is perfect for your business. I got three beautiful young ladies that would like to work in an upscale place like yours. So far, everywhere they've gone, they've always been the club favorites."

"Since I'm a businessman, and it's *always* business, never personal, let me ask you a question. Why do they keep relocating?"

I thought to myself, '*Great question Larry*', but said out loud, "Because usually after a while, the other women get jealous of my girls making all the money. There's three of 'em. I got a 6ft Dominican one, a 5'11" Guyanese and a 5'7" white girl. All of them are beautiful and they already know the ropes."

"Wow. We don't really have anything like that here. Probably all this place is missing, a little diversity. I'd like to try them out. Can you bring them by tonight?"

"Of course I can. See you tonight Mr. Weinstein."

Life is chess, not checkers. You gotta stay five steps ahead of the game. We made good money the past few weeks, but now it's time to double or triple that. Why not? It ain't nothin' but some money. I'm gonna have my girls ready for the world tonight. They gonna bring a breath of fresh air up in this club! *Movin' on up…*

# CHAPTER 30

When I got back to the room, the girls were doing each other's hair and makeup and practicing new dance moves. Their first surprise of the day was Starr; I got two more surprises for them, but I'm gonna wait a little while before I bring those out. I sit at the table, reading the business section of the newspaper, always looking for new opportunities. I let them finish having their l'il girl fun before I pull out my first surprise.

"Hey Ladies, I got a surprise for you."

Amanda spoke first, excitedly. "Another one? What is it papi?" All three are looking at me now, waiting to see what it is. I pull a 3ft long box from under the table. It's a portable stripper pole; an expensive one at that. I put the box on the bed, open it and start to set up the pole in the middle of the floor for them. They're so excited, they just keep hugging me and thanking me.

"You gotta practice how you play," I tell them. "If ya'll gon' do it, be the best at it. I got a passion for being successful and I want ya'll to have the same passion as me, cause at the end of the day, we all we got."

I go out on the balcony to give them some time to get acquainted with their new toy. Now, it's time for me to get into my spiritual realm. I sit down on the lounge chair and start to meditate. I go blank and focus on something bigger than what I know. After about 20/30 minutes, I come back to reality. When I look up, I see Amanda standing right in front of me. She comes closer to me and gave me a hug. She must have seen me through the balcony door and thought that I needed one, and I must have because me and her had a real, deep hug for about two whole minutes. When we let each other go, I tell her to sit down next to me. I look back inside the room, and see the other two still fooling around on the pole, which is a good thing because me and Amanda need these couple of minutes of alone time.

"What made you come out here where I was?"

"I felt somethin' inside that said 'go to him, he needs you.' So, I came!"

"Well, I'm glad that you did. I didn't know I needed you with me until after that hug. Me and you got this connection that *nobody* gon' be able to break."

"I feel it too. I felt it since day one. I'm drawn to you. We're soulmates."

"I don't care how many girls I get, you gon' always be my #1 as long as you don't let no feelings like envy or greed tear us apart. Alright?"

"Alright. I already know that, though," she said, smiling.

"But I'm gonna need you to keep an eye on the other girls. I can't be everywhere with you ladies at all times, so I'm gon' need you to be my eyes and ears when I'm not there. Can you handle that?"

"You ain't even have to tell me to do that, you know I got you."

And I know she means it. "I trust you fully. So, it don't matter who comes and goes, as long as *you* don't ever leave me."

"I'll never leave you, papi. Ain't nothin' out there for me. Plus, we got that genuine love between us that nobody can tear apart. You stuck with me buddy!"

"We stuck with each other, believe it or not!" I laughed too…because it was the truth!

After about fifteen minutes the other girls got bored and saw me and Amanda out on the balcony together. I'm not sure if they liked that or not. Trish knocked on the glass and asked if they could join us. I stood and opened the door for them to come outside. Trish and Starr immediately give me a group hug, so I motion for Amanda to stand up too, and join us. My team is forming nicely. I think this little moment has brought us all a little bit closer. There are only three chairs on the balcony, so Trish sits on my lap, and Amanda and Starr grab a seat. We sit outside for maybe two hours just talking and getting to know each other even better. That's when I reveal to them that we'd be leaving Georgia in exactly two weeks; heading west toward Houston or Dallas. We need to take the WORLD by storm! We don't want any one club or city getting tired of us, we would get tired of them first. My ladies agreed…100%!

# CHAPTER 31

I had my girls in Club Secrets for about a week and a half. They averaged anywhere between $3500- $5000 every night, but that wasn't just from dancing. That included tricking off customers and doing webcam shows. I was really proud of 'em! Everything was on the up and up. Money was flowing good. I had like, $18k, in two separate accounts. I always been good at saving money, especially if I had a particular goal in mind.

Business was going *so* good for us, I felt like I might need me some help. I ain't really too fond of putting people in my game room, I'm a real private person, but I needed assistance. I had my girls going to outcalls and other money-making appointments, and they needed to be on time. I wanted to promote Amanda as my partner/personal assistant, but I really needed her making that money on the other end. Plus, I need her eyes and ears out there in the streets. She's me, when I ain't there. Since I planned on staying in Georgia for maybe another week or so, I decided to look up my cousin, Ant. I haven't seen him since we was about 15. We used to be real, real tight, but you know, sometimes people change when they turn into adults. I don't know exactly what kind of man he's become, but I need some help. I'm only one person, I can't be everywhere at once. My uncle gave me his number at the l'il coming home party they had for me when I first got out. Let me call him and see where his head's at.

Ring ring ring…

"Yo," he said.

"What up cuz, this Saint. What's good wit' it?"

"What's good cuz? I'm just coolin'. What you got goin' on?"

"Shit, I'm just up here in the 'A' shiftin' good…check this out cuz, what you doin' in about 30 minutes?"

"I ain't really got shit goin' on. Why? Wassup?"

"I wanna link up wit' you, grab some lunch or somethin'. I need to talk some business. I might have an opportunity for you."

"Sound tight. Shit been kinda dry out here for me. I need a break! So where you wanna meet me at cuz?"

"Meet me at Zaxby's on Roswell and Midvale. You know where that is, right?"

"Yeah, it's about 15 minutes from me. I'll see you there!"

"Alright. I'm gon' fuck wit' you in about 30 cuz."

Me and Ant hung up. I felt real good about the conversation I just had with my cuz. And this my first cousin, at that. His mom is my dad's sister. He been in Atlanta since he was 15, that means he had eight years to meet and mingle with some of everybody. He should already be plugged in to the scene. Since he's my blood, plus, I always been good at reading people, I know how my cuz Ant is, or how he USED to be, at least. He was always very sneaky and good at manipulating people, even at a young age. I never could really fully trust him, but I'm gonna see if he's changed. And, if he says he's changed, I wanna know how.

I always been a family first type of guy. Family to me isn't always about having the same blood running through your veins. Family, to me, is about who's there when you need them to be. Who you can trust when you feel like you can't trust nobody, and who you can depend on when you're in certain situations. I don't have many people that fit that bill anymore, just Amanda. Plus, I'm always skeptical about bringing another man around my girls. I don't want him getting the wrong idea. I mean, I share; but I don't share *them*. And I will hurt somebody over them. We'll see where this lunch conversation goes. I'm just try'na put some money in his pockets. Off to Zaxby's I go…it's showtime!

# CHAPTER 32

An old boss from an old job, years ago, once told me, "*If you're early, you're on time; if you're on time, then you're late; if you're late, then don't even bother coming!*" That made a lot of sense to me then and I still live by it now, which is why I got to Zaxby's ten minutes after our call ended. I tend to be paranoid, and don't trust too many people, so I sat in the front to peep everybody that was coming in and going out.

Ant walks in about 45 minutes later, typical BPT, but I expected that from him. Like I said, I've known him my whole life. I see him before he sees me. He looks for a second and then comes over to where I'm sitting. He looks like life may have been getting the best of him these days. For a 23-year-old, he just looks kinda tired...worn out...run down. We shake hands and give each other a hug. I start off with, "How's everything goin' for you out here, cuz?"

"I mean, shit kinda up and down. You take the good with the bad. How long you been in town and what brings you to the 'A'?"

Before I answer any of his questions, I watch his body language to see if he's acting nervous or unsure of himself. He seems cool, I guess...."I'm just passing through, actually. I'm on my way out west, just here try'na get my cash up a lil'. I been out here about two months or so."

"Damn cuz. You been here for two months and you just now getting at me?" He shakes his head, "You ain't right Saint. But we past that now. I'm glad to see you bouncing back since you been out. You always been 'bout yo' business."

"Sorry 'bout that cuz. You know I move in silence, like a thief in the night." The waitress came and took our order. I ordered a ten-piece lemon pepper chicken wings special with a glass of water. Ant ordered a spicy chicken burger with onion rings and a Pepsi. After she left, we get back into our conversation, "Lemme ask you this, Ant, and be straight up wit' me. What kind of shit you into? How you gettin' money out here these days?"

"You know me Saint, I always keep me SOME kinda hustle goin' on. Right now I'm sellin' weed and coke, but that shit been kinda slow, so I'm really livin' off my baby mama right now. Feel me?"

"I feel you. What if I say I got a way for you to make $500-$800 per day, and all you have to do is drive for me. Nothin' illegal." When I said that, I saw his face light up like he hit the Powerball jackpot! "Damn right, I'm on that cuz! But, what all I gotta do cause it sounds too good to be true?"

"I need you to drive my girls to they dates, appointments, and whatever else they got goin' on. They runnin' me ragged. I'm only one person and I need some help," I said looking at him, serious as hell!

"I'll help you cuz, whateva you need from me, I got you! This the lil' break I been needin' for a minute!" I see dollar signs in his eyes.

"Listen, I'm gon' give you this opportunity to make some money wit' me, but cuz, I'm gonna be honest wit' you; I don't ever bring men around my girls, you gon' be the first one. Don't make me regret this. I love you, but mess with money or my women, it'll be a problem. I don't play about them." I let that sink in for a second before I went on. "Oh yeah, if you gon' drive my girls around, I got a couple of rules."

"What's the rules cuz?"

"First off, while you driving them, you don't need to talk to them at all. They'll give you the address to where they going, but all that small talk; that's a negative. Second, I'm gon' need you to mind your business and stay outta mine. I'm paying you for a job, and I'm paying you pretty well, at that. As long as we got that understood, we gon' be good. Alright?"

"Alright cuz, I got you. We ain't gon' have no problems."

We finish up our lunch and catch up on family and old friends for 'bout another hour and a half, when I look at my watch and notice time ticking away. Time to end this. We get up, shake hands and go our separate ways. I got my driver; now I can focus on more important things. Even after my meeting with Ant, I still wasn't 100% trusting of him, so I'm gonna always keep a close eye on him. I'll give him enough rope to see if he hangs his self.

# CHAPTER 33

I drop the news on the girls about the new driver that I hired. I also give them the rules on how they should conduct themselves when around other men, but *especially* around men who I'm bringing into our circle. This will be my first time doing this and I didn't want *any* misunderstanding. Amanda, I knew from the gate was my rib, my right hand, she is the one that would never betray me. Me and her have something like a marriage between us. We both promise certain things to each other till death do us part; that's why I didn't mind leaving the girls in certain situations if she was around. She's in charge of the girls and she takes her leadership role very serious.

"Ladies, I know I shouldn't have to tell ya'll this, but when I bring this new driver in today, I don't wanna hear anything about ya'll exchanging numbers with him or even small-talkin'. I mean, in reality, what ya'll got to small-talk about? The only thing you need to say to him is the address, so he can put it in the GPS and that's it. Ya'll got it?" They all nodded. "And even though this my first cousin, I don't trust him like that. I don't really trust no man at all, not around ya'll. And it ain't got nothin' to do with insecurity, it's just a matter of precaution, cause I don't wanna have to hurt or kill nobody 'bout ya'll...but I will if I have to." I look them each in the eye for a few seconds so they would know I was for real. "And oh yeah, ya'll don't have my permission to have sex with *nobody* for free. Ain't no such thing as free sex with nan' one of my women, I ain't havin' it! *Everybody* is a customer. Got it?" They nodded, then Starr said, "We got it Saint baby, but you taught us better than that. We ain't fuckin' *nothin'* for free! If it don't make dollars, it don't make sense!"

"Right," I said.

I had the girls get their schedules together so that when Ant came later on that night, they'd be ready to go. Their schedules were kinda tight, too. Amanda was dancing till 3am. Trish had three outcalls from 9pm till about 2am, at three different locations. Starr had two outcalls from 10pm till 1am, then she gotta be back at the room and get online for a couple of cyber-sex sessions. Ant would be here any minute, so I go over the game plan one more time and tell them to call me when or if they need me. I turn to Amanda, "*I'm* taking you to work. I'll be in there with you for a couple of hours, then I'm gon' go handle some business, but I'll be back in time to pick you up."

"Alright papi."

I tell the other two girls not to give the driver any money. He'll get paid directly from me. Organization is the key to making this work smoothly, like it's been so far.

Five minutes later there's a knock at the door. I answer it and Ant walks in. We shake hands and when he sees the girls, his eyes get wide. You could tell he was try'na keep his composure, but he couldn't hide his excitement. I lead him by the shoulder over to the balcony so we can go over the plans for the night. I briefly introduce him to the girls as we walk through. We are outside and close the door behind us.

"How you doin' tonight cuz?" I ask him.

"I'm good. I'm just ready to get to work!" "Okay. Here's they schedules." I hand him a sheet of paper with all of the info he needs for the night, for Trisha and Starr.

"OK. I got it!"

"If you need anything, or if you get lost, call me. When it's time to get paid, I'll handle that. Talk to me, not them."

"Alright."

"One last thing, Ant...," I pause and he's looking at me straight in the eye, "...please, please, PLEASE don't try me. Now, we ain't gon' have this conversation no more."

"I got you cuz. Let's get to this money!"

OK. He says he's ready to get this money, and I'm gonna give him the opportunity to do that with me. What he don't know, is that my girls are fully trained and capable of seeing when something ain't right, so I'm gon' just sit back and watch how this whole thing plays out. Hopefully, he won't disappoint.

# CHAPTER 34

The first night went about as well as it could. Amanda made a killing at the club; almost three grand by 2am, so she got off a little early. I was already there and waiting, as I promised I would be. She made me proud, like she always does. It was the other two that I was concerned about. This was their first time going out without me, but they stood up in the paint! Each of them did they thang! Between the outcalls and cyber-dates, Starr made like $3800. That's the best night she's had since she been wit' us! This was a huge step for her and I let her know how proud I was. Now my girl Trish always steps up to the plate. She made $4300 in a couple of hours of work. Trish knows how to get that extra money out they ass!

Overall, I'd call it a great night! They did so good, I decided to give them the next day off. I ain't have no problems out of Ant, he ain't even hafta call me; not one time. Good job cuz!

Now that all my girls are in the room safe and sound, it's time to go check cuz in the parking lot, to pay him for his services. Since I decided to give the ladies the day off tomorrow, that means that Ant was off, too. I hopped in his car. He was inside smoking a blunt that smells like it's laced with cocaine. But he off the clock now, so that ain't none of my business.

"You did good cuz, I appreciate it."

"Anytime. So, what time do we start tomorrow?"

"I gave the girls tomorrow off. They worked kinda hard tonight. I'm gon' need you the day after. Cool?"

"Cool."

I went in my pocket and pulled out about $1000. I only owed him $500, but since he did good and my girls ain't complain, I gave him $700 from that. A $200-dollar bonus. I wanted to keep him happy, too. He would've had to sell a lot of weed and other drugs to get that kind of money in three or four hours, and it was all legal…kinda. I counted out the money, in his face, and handed it to him. I was really trying to gauge his facial expression when I paid him. He seemed satisfied, *almost* happy. But there was also a look I detected that said, "*If I get paid THIS, I wonder what YOU get.*" I've seen that look before, that's why I know it so well. But I ain't say nothin'. He folds it and puts it away. I say to him, "That's what we agreed on, plus a bonus since there's no work tomorrow. You alright wit' that?" He hesitated slightly, "Yeah, this good cuz. 'Preciate it."

See...that's what's wrong with people nowadays. Instead of you just being grateful for what you got, you too busy try'na count my pockets.

You can't live your life like that! And that's why I'm in business by myself. It's too easy for men and women to develop animosity, jealousy, greed and hate. It's just too easy. But I'll keep my mouth shut right now and just observe and kill 'em with kindness. I have too many people depending on me to be successful. But what cuz ain't know was that his facial expression turned me off so much, that I had to ask him, *again*, "*You sure* you good cuz? I'm just try'na keep you eatin' wit' me. Shit gon' get greater later, feel me?"

"Yeah I'm good cuz, we straight." He just helped me make up my mind about taking him out west with me when we leave here. He ain't going. I don't need any of that negative energy following me around. I love him, but I love *me* more. But for the next week or so, I'll let him make some more money off of me.

Me and him shake hands again as I get out his car. I watch him pull away, then I walk over to my truck. I get in and start thinkin' about how am I gon' shake this dude without him knowing that he being shook. After about 10 minutes, it comes to me; I know how to lose his ass. I'm gonna just tell him that I got some kind of family emergency with my boys. I'll tell him I'll be back when I take care of the situation, but I just never come back. I ain't gon' change my number and I'm gon' answer the phone every time he calls. I know how to handle dudes like him. You have to make them feel like they won.

I also got a surprise for the ladies. You know I'm full of surprises. Me and the girls going to the gun range. I'm getting them registered and licensed guns in their names. It's better to be safe than sorry out here. I'm just try'na stay ahead of the game.

# CHAPTER 35

Around 11am the next morning, I wake the girls up and I tell them the good news. #1; that they did a good job and they would be off today and #2; that I need them to get dressed cause we're going to the gun range to purchase guns for all three of them. Their eyes get wide and they start screaming and jumping around. I was a convicted felon, so I can't legally own a gun in my name, but that don't mean I don't have one. After all, if you're gonna be in the streets, you gotta be able to survive.

I wait on the balcony while the girls got ready. There's three of them, so the prep time is three times as long! Usually they just all jump in the shower together, so that helps a little bit. While I'm out here, I think to myself, *look how far I've come.* I still have a lot of work to do, and I can't afford to get complacent, cause I know it could all be taken away at any moment. I must have been daydreaming for a while, because I didn't even hear the girls calling my name.

"Earth to Saint! Snap out of it!" Trish says, as she put her arm around my neck.

"OK!" I come out of my daze. "Let's do this!"

The ride to the gun range doesn't take long at all. The girls are chatting it up, like girls do, and I'm in my own lil' world, as usual. We pull up twenty minutes before scheduled. We all get out the truck and make our way to the entrance. I go up to the receptionist and ask for Will, the owner. She goes to the back and re-appears with a tall, skinny white man; almost my height, but not quite. He walks over to me and we shake hands and introduce ourselves to each other. I can only imagine the thoughts in his head, but this is business, so I really don't care. He tells us all to follow him. Now shit is about to get fun!

We walk over to the showcase so they can choose their guns. Starr goes first. I tell her to pick out whichever one catches her eye. After ten minutes of looking, she points out one of the biggest guns in the display! It's an all chrome Glock 40. This gun is damn near bigger than she is! Me and Will give each other a look, but don't say nothing. She says, "Can I see that one?" Will unlocks the case and hands her the gun. Her eyes light up. She turns it from side to side, and even points it in the air. She has a huge smile on her face when she says, "I got the one I want!"

Next is the baby girl, Trish. I know her and I know she's gonna pick the smallest one she can find; she's a girly-girl.

She's pacing the display case for about five minutes, then she calls me over. "Saint! I want this one!" She's pointing at a pink Beretta, and just like I thought, it's the smallest one in the case...but it'll still kill you. We both laugh because she knows that I figured she'd pick that one! I hand it to Will along with Starr's choice, and tell her she did a good job.

Last but not least is Amanda, my protégé. All of them are my girls, but this one here, she knows a little bit more 'bout me than the rest. As a matter of fact, she knows almost everything. She knows my first and last name, my home base in Fort Lauderdale, my kids' names...she knows when I'm mad, disappointed, or unsure. Basically, *she knows me.* And I know her, too. So much so, that when we stroll up and down looking at the different guns, I knew which one she was gonna pick, probably before she did. Why? Because she's more like me than the others. So when I do a double take at the all-black 9mm Ruger, just a little bigger than the size of her palm, with the built-in laser and scope on it, I know it's the one. But I'm not gon' help her decide. She has to do it on her own. It was gon' be *her* gun, but for *our* protection. First, she walks right past it, then 20 seconds later comes back to it. A second time...goes and comes back.
I say, "Yeah baby that's the one, I feel it too. Stop fighting it." She never takes her eyes off of it as she speaks to me and says, "Yep that's it papi." Will takes it out the display case and hands it to her. It's like love at first sight, for the both of us.

This piece is perfect for Amanda. You wouldn't know she was strapped unless she told you. The gun's small, but it'll kill you. It may look like a toy, but it's dead serious. She keep people on her scope and the laser makes her accurate. She isn't gonna miss. Amanda seems gullible, like she's a pushover cause she don't talk much, unless spoken to. I always tell her the loudest one in the room is usually the weakest link in the room. She is my muse; my best student. When she picked it up, she gave it a name out the gate. She names her gun *Midnight*, because of how black it is and how hard it is to see her coming with it. I get each of them two boxes of ammo and we proceed to the shooting area. I wanna see what they got.

Trish handles her little pink gun like a professional. She even hits the bull's-eye a couple of times. I know in a few days, when she finally gets her concealed weapons license, she gonna carry that little gun everywhere. And only pull it out if she feels like she's in danger.

Starr's gun is not quite what I would have picked for her. I kinda think it's a little too big, but she knows how to handle it. My problem is her attitude. She don't have an attitude towards *me*, it's just that quick temper that she got; I'm kinda afraid that if she gets in an argument or disagreement with a client or even a regular person, that she's gonna pull out her gun. And not just pull it out, but shoot it. That girl has no fear. She, by far, is the toughest outta all my girls. But she's a sweetheart. She soft underneath all that toughness. I just don't wanna be spending tens of thousands of dollars on a lawyer fighting a murder case for her. But it wouldn't have been right for the other girls to have a gun and not her. So I'll just hafta trust her decision-making skills.

We spend over five hours at the gun range that day. Surprisingly, the girls picked up very quickly on how to load, handle, and shoot their guns. They make me proud. It seems like all three of the girls did a good job of picking a gun that they felt comfortable with. I felt confident after leaving the gun range that day, that if it had to go down in a shootout between my girls and the bad guys; my girls would prevail. Amanda was the best shooter of the three, but I'd never tell them that. The cashier tells us the licenses should arrive in about six days.

On our way back to the room we decide to grab an early dinner. We stop by *Gladys Knight's Soul Food Cuisine*. This was our first time eating there. I had always heard this was the best soul food joint in all of Georgia. We get a booth near the window. Everybody places their orders. While we wait for the waitress to bring the food, we chop it up a lil' bit. I know the waitress probably finds it strange to see a black guy eating with three strikingly beautiful women of three different races.

"Listen ladies, I wanna explain to ya'll why I bought ya'll these guns. They are strictly for the sole purpose of protection when I ain't around. Now, that don't mean pullin' em out every chance you get. These are weapons. Guns kill people. Now I don't mind if you kill somebody that's threatening your life or trying to rape or harm you; as long as you know that there's consequences behind your actions. I need ya'll to carry these everywhere y'all go. Nobody, and I mean *nobody* needs to know y'all got guns unless you finna use it. And another thing, if anybody talking about robbing me, I want you to kill 'em, without hesitation. That's why I bought them for y'all. Because if somebody rob and steal from me, they rob and steal from us all. I just been having a strange feeling, deep down inside, that there's outside people watching us, waiting for us to slip up and take what we done worked so hard for.

By the time we get out west, we should have enough money for at least a 4 or 5-bedroom house. A big house, on a hill somewhere. We on the right track, I just need y'all to have my back like I got ya'll front."

"I got you papi. If anybody tries something I'ma put a hole in his ass the size of a golf ball!" Amanda said. "I'm for real."

Starr said, "They think I'm mean now; let somebody try to take something from any one of us, it's gonna be World War Three in this bitch." We all laughed, then Trish made a gun sign with her finger and said, "King Kong ain't got shit on us!" We busted out laughing again because she was dead ass serious. This hard work that these girls put in, ain't nobody gonna take it.

# CHAPTER 36

The next few days came and went so fast. Even though things were going smoothly, I was still feeling a lil' uneasy. Maybe I'm just paranoid.... I was still handling my business as far as doing what I said I was gonna do money-wise for my kids. $1000 a week is a lot of money for anybody, so no one was complaining! The gun range called and let me know the licenses would be ready tomorrow, which couldn't come fast enough!

The money was flowin'. The customers must have known that we were leaving town soon, because they been spending extra dough the last few days. In the span of five or six days, we brought in about $46k, collectively. I split that into two different accounts and I kept 10 grand in the room safe. In addition, I always kept about $2000 cash on me at all times.

I had like four more girls approach me to join the team. Don't get me wrong, they were bad, it's just not ladylike for *them* to come to *me*. I mean, it doesn't offend me or anything, I just can't peep the angle. I'm used to doing the chasing. I feel like it could have been a setup. Maybe somebody who's envious of me and my team, so they try'na send they girls in to infiltrate my camp. So, at this point, I ain't taking nobody else from the Atlanta area...period!

I think the time has come for us to leave Georgia. We made the money we needed to make here. We did better than I could have even imagined, but the next location gon' be even better than this. I can feel it. Tomorrow, after we go pick up the guns for the ladies, I'm gon' start planning our next move: Houston. I'm not gon' tell Ant anything. In two days, all of a sudden, we just gon' be gone! Family emergency...he'll understand. And if he don't, oh well! I'll tell the girls the play tonight when they get off work. Or maybe I'll just shoot 'em all a text message now; this way they'll know to hustle a lil' harder these next two nights.

TO: Amber, Starr, Trish

"I'm gon need ya'll to pack up the room. We finna hit the road Sat morning. We on to the next city. Move in silence. Our business ain't everybody business. I'll be there to pick ya'll up at 3:50 (am)."

SEND

Cool. Now the girls know what the next move is. All I really need to do now is lay low, and pay cuz what I owe him. I'm gon' even give him a nice bonus. A lil' cherry on top! I don't want him feeling any type of way when I leave without telling him. I mean, I'm a grown-ass man and I don't have to tell another grown-ass man shit! But when I first brought him on, I may have slipped and told him he could go with us when we shifted out west. But plans change. I don't trust him.

# CHAPTER 37

Friday 9:35 am

I wake up to my phone ringing. Trish is in the bed next to me and Amanda and Starr are in the other bed.

Ring ring ring...

"Hello?" It's a number I don't have saved in my phone, and not too many people have my number.

"Good morning. This is Will from Supreme Gun Range. I am calling to inform you that the licenses have come in for the three firearms that you purchased last week. You can come pick up your guns whenever you like!"

*Perfect.* Everything was coming together. My girls are now licensed to carry concealed guns. I feel a lil' less paranoid now.

"Oh, OK. Thank you very much Will. We'll be there in an hour."

I jump out of bed and go take me a hot shower before the ladies use all the hot water. Today is a big day for all of us. I finish my shower, brush my teeth and put on some clothes. Now, it's time to wake the girls.

"Ladies. Ladies. Wake up. Wake up. Wake up!! I got a surprise for ya'll!!"

They rose slowly, one at a time. Once I see that they all up, I make my announcement: "The guns are ready! So ya'll get up, hit the shower, and hurry up and get dressed. Ya'll got one hour. We got a lot of stuff to do today."

I enjoy seeing the looks on they faces when the news starts to really sink in. They're more excited than me. Amanda speaks first, "I miss Midnight already, and we haven't even known each other long." Starr starts jumping up and down on the bed like she's eight years old, "Let's go get my baby!" Trish speaks calmly, with a big grin on her face, "It's time to come home to mama."

Even with two of the girls taking a shower together, they had used a little more than the one hour I gave them to get ready.

It seems like I'm doing 100 mph to get there. I ain't ever got anywhere that fast before today. I'm excited!

By the time we get there, the manager has each gun in an individual box. The girls open each box in amazement. They each have their own lil' piece of power. I let them play around with them a little, we pack up the two boxes of ammo they each have. I pay for it all and we head out. They're ready for the world now!

Now we're hungry so we go to a local diner, not too far from the gun range. There are smiles on all my girls' faces. I can tell that they're excited by the new challenges and adventures we're about to encounter. I'm still leaning towards Houston, but Dallas is a good option as well. I decide to get their opinions on it. "So ladies, should our next move be Dallas or Houston?" I know they'll give me an honest answer. And bottom line, if there's anywhere that they don't like, then we ain't going! "It's cool." "Wherever you wanna go." "We trust your judgment papi" …is basically the answer. I pretty much already know that they just wanna go wherever I wanna go, but I still like to involve them every step of the way.

We talk about everything while we're sitting at the table. I tell 'em I need the whole room empty; don't leave ANYTHING behind. With three of them getting the shit together, it won't take long to clear out. They know I keep money in the safe, just not how much. I always make it a priority to keep all three of their business separate. They know not to discuss money with each other.

"Alright. So this what we gon do; We gonna head to Houston first. That's where our next big money stop gon' be. After we chill there for a few weeks, we should be about

$250k strong, so by the time we get to Vegas, we should be able to buy a nice house for all of us. Everybody gonna have their own room and maybe even bathroom! Once we get to our permanent destination, we gon' pick up two more girls, and make us a complete five. I don't really think we need more than that. I need to be able to keep my eye on ya'll. OK? So that's where we at. This our last night of work in Atlanta, so let's make it a good one! And remember, nobody knows we leaving, and I wanna keep it like that. Cool?"

They all shook their heads in agreement. *Cool.*

# CHAPTER 38

It's 8:15pm, almost time for my girls to go to work. We already went over the schedules for the night, right now we're just waiting on Ant to come pick them up. He'll be here any minute, I'm sure. As usual, Trish and Starr would be riding with him for the evening. I like to follow the same routine so that things can always go as smooth as possible. Everybody knows it's Ant's last night, except for Ant! Just because we're related, that don't make us 'family'. My girls are more family to me now, but he served his purpose. Plus, he made some money, so he can never say that I ain't ever do anything for him; that'd be a lie!

There's a knock at the door. I look out the peep hole, and it's him. Ten minutes late, but it's cool. I plan on giving him a $1500 bonus tonight, cause in reality, he done a good job of driving for me. I let him in. "What's good wit' it cuz? You alright?" I ask him, as I give him a handshake. "Yeah. I'm good. Ya'll bout ready?" The whole time he's shaking my hand, he never gives me eye contact. He's looking everywhere in the room, except at me. Maybe it's just me being paranoid again…I guess. "Yeah, we ready. Let's roll ladies."

All of us leave the room at the same time. Two vehicles heading in two different directions, all with the same goal: money. I'm going to the club with Amanda, like I always do, and Ant is taking the other two on they outcalls and other scheduled dates or last minute calls. We all set for the night!

About two hours later, I'm in the club with Amanda, enjoying the scene and indirectly saying my 'good-byes'. As soon as I order my second glass of Remy, my phone rings. It's Ant.

"Cuz…"
"What's up?" I ask him.

"Ay…I was at the l'il spot over here waiting for Starr to finish up with her customer and all of a sudden her phone dies or somethin'. I ain't sure, but she ain't answering now, it's goin' straight to voicemail and I don't know which door she went in. We already done been here for over an hour and this was supposed to be a quick 30-minute call."

Damn. This that BS I be talkin' 'bout! "Where Trish at?" I sobered up immediately, and now I'm pissed off!

"I dropped her off to the room. She say she was finna do her cyber thing for the rest of the night."

"So, what you need from me?"

"I need your help! These yo' girls!"

"Man. Fuck. Send me the address to where you at right now. I'm on my way."

# CHAPTER 39

I tell Amanda I'll be back, jump in my truck and head down Highway 285 doing 100mph trying to get to my girl. Truth be told, Starr is a real asset to the team. She been making good money since she been with me and I'm responsible for her. When I tell my girls I ain't gon' let nothing happen to them, I mean it!

The GPS says I have five more minutes until I reach my destination. I keep saying to myself over and over, "Don't let nothing happen to my girl. PLEASE don't let nothing happen to my girl." Despite whatever wrong I may or may not be doing out here in this world, I don't view myself as a bad person. I have a very big heart, and right now I'm worried sick.

I pull up to the address and immediately get mad at myself because I had let her come to a place so run-down and abandoned looking. They look like some condos or townhouses, or somethin'…but deserted. There's only four cars in the parking lot, one of them is Ant's. Soon as I put my truck in Park and get out, Ant gets out his car...with a gun in his hand.

"Don't move and keep your hands where I can see 'em."

In my mind, I'm like, "*Ain't this a bitch! All that I done for this broke mu'fucca!!*" But to my surprise, I ain't even surprised. I kinda expected this all along. I said to him, "Damn cuz. What's this about?"

"Don't 'cuz' me. What the fuck you mean what's this about? You already know what this is. I need that cash *cuz*."

I keep my hands in the air, and my eyes on him, "So this how you gon' do me? We grew up from the dirt! Your mom is my dad's sister! I put money in yo' pockets, now you wanna rob me? I can't believe this fuck ass shit!"

"Man...fuck all that shit. We ain't kids no mo'. It's every man for himself. You tried to pigeon-feed me. All that money you be makin', and you wanna pay me $500 a night? Fuck that! Now I want it ALL. And please don't make me kill you, cause I will."

Those were the words coming out his mouth as he's looking me in my face with bloodshot red eyes. I see death in his face, but I ain't never been scary, so I hold my ground. Desperate times call for desperate measures. Time to think quick. That's when he hit me with the alley-oop play. With three seconds left on the clock, he pulls out his ace in the hole. He says, "Come on out babe," and taps the hood of the car. The passenger door opens. I think it's gonna be a car full of dudes with guns, ready to shoot me if I move. But it's not. When the door fully opens, my heart drops. It's Starr, and she got her gun pointed at me. The same gun I just bought her. This bitch! But I play dumb. "Damn baby, I'm glad you alright, I thought somethin' happened to you." I always felt like I'd make a great actor, so this was the perfect time to rehearse.

She doesn't buy it. "Baby my ass! You been using me ever since I met you. You're a manipulator, so I'm ridin' wit' Ant now. It's over between you and me. Fuck ya! But thanks for the gun. It sure came in handy!"

It was hard for me to hide my anger and disappointment, but I did my best. They want to kill me. Right now. But I know they won't do anything without getting the money first. I still got my hands in the air when Ant says, "Where's the cash?" We're probably about six to eight feet away from each other. I have to come up with a plan real quick.

"I got about $15k in my pocket and another couple grand in the truck. Just don't kill me cuz." I take one arm out the air and start to reach in my pocket.

"I told you, don't call me cuz. And move slow while you go in those pockets buddy. And don't do nun' stupid. On second thought, please...*please* do somethin' stupid!"

I say, "Chill. I'm not." I put my hand in my front right pocket and pull out a wad of cash. While I have my hands out where he can see them, with the money in my right hand, I throw it all in the air and then I run in the direction of my truck. Starr yells out, "Shoot his ass!!!"

I don't know how good of a shot he is, but I know how good Starr was...deadly. And she done came too far now to turn back. But I ain't really have time to focus on her.

I'm running and ducking behind cars trying to make it back to the entrance of the cul de sac we were in. I decide to make a run for the entrance; I ain't really have a choice. So I take off, trying to stay as low as possible cause I know how hard it is to hit a moving target. I hear Ant yelling, "He's try'na get away! Get him!" I'm in a zone now, then I start hearing the shots. *Pop! Pop! Pop! Pop!* These motherfuckas really tryin' to kill me! Bullets flying over my head, I keep saying to myself, "*I wanna live. I wanna live. Your kids need you Saint.*" I'm almost at the entrance when I hear two more pop sounds. Then my back and my leg start to burn. I run about another fifteen feet when I drop like a sack of potatoes. My shirt and my pants are wet. Why the hell is my body on fire? My head is spinning and I can't tell if I'm conscious or not. I try to get up and run the other twenty feet to make it to the 24-hr corner store I saw when I first got here, but my legs feel like bricks. I use whatever upper body strength I have left to pull myself toward the lights. I can see lights…just a lil' bit more. I'm almost there. Now I start to see flashes of my grandma's face. Then of King and Zion, smiling and laughing. I can't die. My kids need me….

I guess all the gunshots brought out the people who was in the store. I look up and see what I thought was God and his Angels but, in reality, is just the owner of the store standing over me, with three of his customers. I reach my hand up and he grabs it and says, "Don't move. Help is on the way. Can you hear me? Stay with me." I pray to God while I lie on my back, crying. My body's on fire. I turn my head to the right and see Ant's car passing by. I wanna yell out, "There's the guy who shot me!" but no words come out, so I try to get up and then realize there's no feeling in my feet. Then, I black out…

# CHAPTER 40

## Part Three: NEW BEGINNINGS

I wake up with tubes running through my veins and out of my nose. *Why the fuck am I in the hospital? What's happened to me?* I vaguely recall having a nightmare about guns and being shot, and...wait...*why the fuck can't I feel my toes? They aren't moving!* And my back is killing me. I look down and see my left leg bandaged up. I lay my head back down on the pillow and try to relive in my head what the fuck happened to me! I really can't believe this shit! I know this ain't happen to me...not *me! Man, what the hell am I gon' tell my kids? They moms?* I start to get depressed, then I hear the toilet flush. I look around the room and spot the bathroom door and guess who walks out? Amanda!

"Hey papi," she says, smiling. She rushes over to me and gives me a big kiss and hug. She has tears in her eyes, "I'm so glad you're awake. It's been a *long* three days."

"What you mean three days? What day is it?"

"It's Monday. You been sleep for three days papi."

"What the fuck?" I paused, then, "Where's Trish?" As soon as I ask the question, Trish walks in the door. "Hey Saint baby! Welcome back! We gon' get those mutha fuckas, don't worry!"

"Yeah," I say, "payback's a bitch. So, what I miss? How ya'll know what happened? Where ya'll been stayin'?"

Amanda speaks first, "When you didn't come back to pick me up from work, I knew something was wrong. You've *never* not shown up. So I called the police station and then the local hospital to see if they knew anything, and I found you! I still can't believe that bitch Starr did something like this after all you've done for her!"

"How do you know all that?" I ask because if I been out of it for three days, then I obviously ain't been talking to no one, including the police!

"I don't know if it's the meds they have you on or what, but you been talking in your sleep!

Me and Trish been here with you since you got here, and taking notes!" She taps her purse and says, "We stay strapped because of you papi. Don't know who to trust anymore."

Then Trish speaks. "One of the bullets hit you in the leg and the other one pierced your spine. The doctor says you're lucky to be alive. So...as of right now, you can't walk." She can't even look right at me. "They're waiting for the swelling to go down before they decide what's next." Then she just breaks down crying. Then Amanda starts crying too!

"What the hell ya'll doin'? This ain't my funeral and this ain't the time to be crying. We got work to do! I ain't on that soft shit! I need ya'll to tighten up!"

They both immediately stop. Then look at each other and started laughing.

"That's better!"

Trish comes and sits on the bed next to me and holds my hand, and looks at me with a serious face, "But for real. We was scared. Real scared. We ain't know what to do. Good thing Amanda held it together. I can't lie, I was losin' it! We caught a cab down here right away. You were in surgery for 16 hours and we been here with you the entire time. We love you. You know that. But...what exactly happened out there?"

I close my eyes for a second to gather my thoughts. Everything becomes crystal clear, "Ant set me up. Him and Starr set me up real good. He called me and told me to meet him at an address cause he couldn't find Starr and he needed my help. So when I got there, he pulled a gun on me. Then Starr hopped out the car and pulled her gun on me too, and they robbed me. When I started to run away, they shot me."

"That's messed up. You took care of both of them. Well, the police came by for a statement while you were out. What you gonna tell 'em when they come back?"

"I ain't givin' no statements. I don't remember nothing. I'm gon' handle all my business in the streets. And ya'll better not say anything either. We gonna handle this as soon as I get back right."

Amanda says, "Damn right we gonna handle that! But for now, just chill, get your legs right. First things first. We need you walking again."

I agreed. "Cool. Check this out. I don't want ya'll doin' nothing routine. I don't want ya'll at the club or nothing till I get back right. I don't trust nobody in these streets right now. We not from around here. Got it?" They both nod.

The doctor walks in about an hour later and introduces himself as Dr. Barnes. We shake hands and he proceeds to read me the analysis on his chart. I have swelling on the fourth and fifth vertebrae. He is honest when he tells me that my chances of walking again are 50/50. I stop him and tell him, "The Devil is a liar." He looks at me and smiles and says he likes my enthusiasm. I tell him I plan on walking in six months or less. He goes on to tell me that he believes in me, which gives me hope. He tells me that my physical therapist will be in to meet me. We shake hands and he leaves. I'm starting to feel better already...

# CHAPTER 41

Thirty minutes later *she* walks in. Who is she, though? She ain't really dressed like a doctor, but she is still somebody important. I can't take my eyes off of her. She's the most beautiful, amazing looking woman I've ever seen. She's slim, with a dark caramel complexion, coke-bottle shape, long hair down the middle of her back and the prettiest white teeth that I've ever seen! I cannot take my eyes off this woman. And her eyes; they have me locked all the way in. They are the sexiest mixture of chestnut brown and determination. We lock eyes and, for a second, I think she feels it too cause there is this electricity she gives off. I am instantly drawn to her. I wonder if she feels the same way? Maybe she does, but just don't know it yet. I want this woman. I *need* this woman. I think I found my future wife! We are just staring at each other for what feels like ten minutes, silent, until I think I hear Amanda say, "Hello! How are you?" Instantly we snap out of our trance.

"Hello. I'm fine. How are you all doing? I'm Ms. Haynes, the physical therapist assigned to our patient here." I immediately see the jealousy on my girls' faces. I mean, my girls are beautiful, but this woman has a different kind of beauty. It's...almost regal. They have the right to be jealous because what they're feeling is on point. I want that woman; not to work for me, but to work *on* me. To love me. To undress me. To marry me. I've heard people say somethin' about 'love at first sight', but I never really believed in it, until now. I am a *firm* believer now. *Sold!* I have found my soulmate. Now, I just gotta see if she feels the same way. One thing is for sure; we got a connection. I can feel it.

The girls introduce themselves, "Hi. I'm Trish."

"And I'm Amanda. Nice to meet you."

"Nice to meet you two, as well." She turns to me, "Now, Mr. Stephon St. Claire...," she calls me by my government name, and I don't even mind. "...it seems like we have a huge mountain to climb with you. Don't be discouraged. But I just want to be honest, we have a lot of work to do so I kinda want to get started right away, if that's OK?"

"Sounds like a plan. Ms. Haynes!" I say.

She leans over me and starts removing the tubes. Her scent drifts up into my nose, putting me back into a trance. After all the tubes are out, she goes to the door and pulls a wheelchair inside the room. She lowers the bed and helps me into the chair. She tells the girls that we'd be back in about an hour and wheels me out the room and down the hallway to the physical therapy training room. There are maybe ten other people in there with they trainers, and I am certainly glad they had their own, cause I ain't sharing mine! God has really been good to me. First, he saves my life, then, he brings me this beautiful woman. She ain't mine yet, but give me time.

There's not very much that I could do since the injury was still very fresh. There was still a lot of swelling, so the only thing I can really do is some stretching. Well, *she* was doing the stretching cause I still couldn't feel my legs. But she was doing an excellent job of bending over and putting her hands on my legs, then my feet; trying to get the blood circulating. I ask her if she thinks this is too soon for any of this since I just got shot a few days earlier, which *still* seems like yesterday to me. She tells me that she didn't want a mental block to develop. Fifty percent of why people are permanently paralyzed is mental. They let their mind win. She says in my case, it's good to get an early start to try to avoid any setbacks. She doesn't want any distractions. That's when she hits me with; "I think your girlfriends are going to slow down your progress. You really need to use this time to focus on yourself." I ain't have a problem with anything she just said. It's more of how she said it; sounded a bit jealous-like to me. And what does she mean 'girlfriends' with an 's'? Was she try'na call me a gigolo? Whatever it is, I kinda like it, so I respond like only I could, "I don't have a girlfriend. Those are my *friends*. But if you feel like they'll slow down my progress, they're gone, cause I'm gonna walk again, and soon. *Trust me*." Her face looks relieved, then she says, "Excellent. Excellent. Now, we're gonna start light. I want you to get into the routine of waking up early in the morning and getting the blood circulating." She's staring me in my eyes and smiling. Time stopped again. Then I snap out of it, "Question? So, are you my permanent therapist, cause I ain't try'na be switchin' people every day. Plus, I like who I got right now. I don't want nobody else."

She blushed and said, "Of course I'm your permanent therapist. You're stuck with me sir! So get ready to see my face every single day for at least the next three months!" We both smiled. I'm just glad she can keep me in good spirits. My girls, Amanda and Trish, are good at that too, but my therapist says they probably won't be good for my recovery, so I gotta break the bad news to them when I get back to the room. They gotta go!

# CHAPTER 42

After the hour was up, Ms. Haynes rolled me back into the room where the girls are waiting for me. She helped me back in the bed, hooked my tubes back up and gave me a side eye like, *you know what you gotta do*. I thank her and give her the same side eye right back! *I know what I gotta do*! She told me she'd see me tomorrow, waved to the girls and left.

The girls are seated near my bed when I tell them that we need to strategize. "First, don't let me being in a wheelchair right now stop this money. I'll bounce back in a couple of months. But for right now, I need you guys to get back on the grind. I need ya'll to go to the room and get all the money and jewelry out the safe. Clean the room out COMPLETELY and then check out. Go to the tow-yard and get my truck. I need ya'll to handle things while I'm in here. You two need to stick together like Siamese twins. Don't let ANYTHING come between ya'll. Just move light, till I get back on my feet. When you have the money and the truck, I want ya'll to get an apartment near here and pay up the rent for six months. I don't want ya'll dancing right now. Ya'll can do dates with your regulars, but no new people. I don't really trust nobody right now. I need ya'll to step up, OK? And get this money! My therapist says that I need this lil' time to focus on me, so just keep me updated on what's going on out there. I'll call ya'll when I need ya'll. Keep your guns on you at all times. If you don't feel right about somethin', don't do it. I need ya'll to call me every day and I don't want no customers at the apartment. Here's the key to the safety deposit box...." I hand the key to Amanda. "It's at First National Bank, Box #1142. All the money that you make while I'm in here, put it in there. Don't keep *any* money at the apartment. Got it?"

"We got this," they both said. They get their things together to leave and each gives me a hug and kiss. Before they walk out the room, I tell them, "Ladies, I love ya'll. Be safe and don't let me down. I'm depending on you two. Call me later!"

"We love you papi and you can count on us!" I can see in Amanda's face that she doesn't wanna go, but I have to get myself right for them. Well, really for me, cause I'm not 100% sure I'm gettin' back in the game. I might've found the woman to take me out this life for good. But first things first...I gotta get these legs workin' again!

The room was quiet and I'm sittin' there contemplating all the 'what ifs'. *What if my legs don't ever work again? What if my girls leave me while I'm rehabbing? What if I never get my confidence back again? What if Ms. Haynes is married? What if Ant comes back to finish the job while I'm in here?* I just let my mind wander for a while. That's how *I* self-heal. I let myself wallow in self-pity for a while before snapping out of it and never doing it again! I'm better than that! One thing that I'm sure of, is that God saved me from getting killed out there so I know he has a bigger calling for me. That's why I know I'm gonna walk again. I'm determined.

But right now it's time to break the news to my kids' moms and my grandma. They are the only *real* family I have. I decide to call Lashonda first. Me and her will never ever get back together again, but she's still the mother of my child so, …I'll make this short and sweet.

Ring ring ring…

"Hello?"

"Wassup Shonda?"

"Nothin'. We at the water park right now. Wassup?"

"OK. Just you and King?"

"Talia and Zion, too. You said you wanted us to get along, so…"

"Well I'm glad you're taking my advice! And it's actually a good thing ya'll together right now. I need ya'll to go somewhere quiet so ya'll can hear me clearly on speaker, alright?"

"Alright." I heard her tell Talia I'm on the phone and want to talk to both of them. After about a minute, she says, "Alright. We're here. What's goin' on?"

"Listen carefully and don't get crazy, but I was shot twice; once in the spine and once in the leg and, as of right now, I'm temporarily paralyzed. I'm going through rehab and it's gon' take a few months to get right again. Don't tell the boys, of course. They too young to understand any of this, anyway." I hear them both crying, then asking if they can come see me.

"I told ya'll to be calm and just chill. I got enough on my plate right now. Don't tell nobody, not even my family. I'll call ya'll back again soon." I hang up the phone feeling worse than when I called, but they have my kids and they need to know what's goin' on with me.

# CHAPTER 43

8:15am the next morning

I don't know why I'm up so early; I'm feelin' good! Maybe because I'm ready to see my girl, Ms. Haynes. I get to see her six days a week, and she should be here in about an hour.

I start smiling cause I know I still got money put up. There's about $94K divided into two different accounts, and I also have another account that nobody knows about. It's one that me and my grandmother share. There's about another $18K in that one. I've never minded sharing that account with my grandma, cause even if she spent every dime in it, it still wouldn't amount to all that she's done for me. She raised me! Plus, no one would ever think to check her account. But she always has her own money, anyway. She's a retired school principal, so she's set.

Even though Ant and Starr shot me, robbed me and tried to kill me; I ain't gonna focus anymore of my attention on them...for now. I need to get my legs back! Ain't no more feelin' sorry for myself. That's over! The nurse already came and washed me down, which was kinda fun, even though I would have preferred Ms. Haynes. I start to drift off in to la la land until someone knocks on the door. "Come in." My day just got even better. It was my boo!

"Hello! Good morning!" she said smiling, trying to melt my heart early in the morning. "How'd you sleep?" I figured out her superpower; direct eye contact!

"Good morning beautiful. I slept good; it could have been great but I was missing one person," I said smiling, giving her back her direct eye contact. I ain't scared of her!

"I bet!" We both laughed.

"Call me Stephon, even though no one's called me that since elementary school. But I want *you* to call me that, if you wouldn't mind."

"Of course I wouldn't mind! I hope you're ready for rehab today!"

"I'm ready for whatever you got for me! I mean...whatever *therapy* you got for me, of course."

"Uhm Hmm...I bet. Let's get you outta this bed, Stephon."

She lowered the bed. I put my arm over her shoulder as she took my left foot and put it on the wheelchair. I caught a whiff of her perfume; she smells like pomegranate and raspberries and all types of sweet-smelling fruit! I ain't wanna take my arm from around her! After she put my other foot on the footrest of the wheelchair, she must have felt it too, cause she looked me in my eyes for a minute. Her face is just inches away from mine; I can smell her shampoo now. She looks down and catches a glimpse of my groin area…I guess SOME things still work! She pulls away, then says, "Whoa playboy! Control yourself!" I could tell she wasn't really offended, but I didn't wanna push it too far on the second day of therapy. That's what my problem is; I go zero to 100, I don't really have a middle gear. So sometimes I get myself in trouble. But one thing I'm sure of…me and Ms. Haynes got a connection.

"My fault. That thing has a mind of its own. It must know a beautiful woman is around…Ms. Haynes, can I ask you a question? Are you married? Please say no!" She's slowly pushing me down the hall to the PT room when she gives me the answer I've been waiting for, "No sir, I am not. Why?"

"Because if you were married, your husband is 'bout to be in a lot of trouble, because I feel like I found the woman of my dreams. I would hafta take you from him. But since you're not married, we don't have to worry about that!"

She laughs. "Damn, you're confident. Just because I'm not married, doesn't mean that I'm not seeing anyone. And *who* says you're my type? And another thing, I don't date, nor have I ever dated, a street dude! I like my men free! I don't date thugs, boo boo. And I don't date men who get shot every other week. Sorry!"

"Ms. Haynes, lemme get this straight…what I got out of all of that, is that you're fascinated by me, you're intrigued to learn more about me, and even though I got shot, that doesn't make me a bad guy. Oh yeah, and you would LOVE to be Mrs. St Claire. Am I correct?"

"Umm…not at all. As a matter of fact, you're 100% incorrect! But, hey, we all gotta dream, eh?" I got her blushing again. And laughing. Another word for it all; flirting!

We finally get to the therapy room and, again, it's full. We start out the same way as yesterday; she helps me out the wheelchair, and lays me on the mat. We start stretching, but this time is more intense than the first time. We ain't flirting, we ain't laughing…we're sweating! She's really trying to get my legs working again. And I appreciate it!

This full throttle-type stretching and exercising goes on for another three weeks. As the swelling starts to go down, the feeling starts to come back a little. I have movement in my big toe on my right foot and in my two little toes on the left foot. Things are looking up. Ms. Haynes was just as excited as I was about the feeling starting to return. One day after our normal therapy session, we stay an extra hour. We are the only two left in the room. We're both sitting on the mat, on the floor, facing each other, drinking bottled water. I ask her, "What's your first name? You got me calling you Ms. Haynes like you some school teacher or somethin'! I mean, if you don't mind me knowing."

She smiles that beautiful smile again, "I don't mind. My name is Kelly." She's acting kind of shy. It's a first!

"Listen Kelly; I ain't 100% yet, but I'm getting there with your help. First off, I wanna thank you for everything you've done, so far. May I ask you something else?"

"It depends on what it is, cause you ask a lot of damn questions wit' your nosey self!"

We both laugh at that. But then I get dead serious, "When I get myself together, can I take you out sometime?" I don't play when it comes to my heart.

She gives me that cute little grin that I love, "Well, I don't know about that. What will your two lil' girlfriends say?"

"What I said last time when you tried to slide that lil' remark in? I'm single. Those are my *friends* that just want to make sure that I am OK. They care about me. Now I'm try'na be *your* friend and care about *you*!"

"Funny! One thing's for sure, you're very persistent. I kinda like that. I just don't know if I could ever trust a guy like you, though."

"And why would you say that? I haven't lied to you about anything. I'm an open book. Anything you wanna know, I'll tell you." I'm looking her straight in the eyes.

She thought for a second. "OK, Mr. Open Book, why are *you* single?"

"Because I haven't found a woman who can hold a conversation for more than thirty minutes about something more than her hair or nails!"

"OK. Why are you hanging around two women? Where's your family?"

"I told you, we friends! Them girls just piss you off, huh?" This is actually kinda cute to me! "I'm from down south; Ft Lauderdale. That's home base; gramma's house. I don't really have any family here. My mother and father passed away...that's about it."

"Oh. Sorry to hear that. You got kids?"

"Yeah. I got two little boys, both three years old. Their names are King and Zion and they all I have in this world."

She smiled, "Aww...that's so sweet. So, let me ask you a question, where do you see yourself in five years?"

Ha! A familiar question! "In five years, I should own me a couple of businesses and be traveling around the world with my wife or girlfriend or somebody special."

"Sounds nice. What do you do for a living?"

Damn. I hate that question. "Since I've been honest with you since I've met you, I'm gonna continue being honest. I'm a manager and, sometimes, I'm a collections agent." I distorted the truth a little bit. Everybody wants the truth, but not everybody can handle it! The look on her face let me know she wasn't 100% believing my occupation, but hey, what can I do?

"Mmm Hmm...I hear you. So, you wanna ask me anything?"

"Yep! Will you marry me?" We both burst out laughing.

"You get straight to the point, don't you!"

We chilled for maybe another hour, just small talking. We got a lot closer today. So I was right when I thought that we both felt the connection. I knew it! But I can tell this gon' be different than any other girl I ever been with. This one is gonna take time; it ain't gon' be no overnight thing. But all I got is time right now, so why not?

She rolled me back to my room and helped me back on to the bed, so I get one more time to smell her hair. I want that scent stuck in my brain! Things are looking up, as of lately. Three of my toes are working plus I might have me a date when I get back on my feet again!

# CHAPTER 44

Amanda and Trish found an apartment about twenty minutes from the hospital. A nice lil' two-bedroom, second floor, furnished spot for $800 per month. They have the truck, so they're able to get around town when they need to. Money is flowing, as usual. Not as much, but it's still flowing. I talk to them both every day, so I know exactly what Amanda's putting in the safety deposit box each day.

I have Trish do a lil' detective work and she finds an old friend of mine from college, my homie OJ, that I heard was out here now. When she finds him, I tell her to pass my number along to him. A few days later...

Ring ring ring...

"Hello?" I'm confused because it's an unsaved number.

"Wassup homie? I hear you done went and got yourself shot."

"Man, who the fuck is this?"

"Man, this OJ! What the hell you done got yourself into?"

I'm shocked to hear from my homie. I knew that Trish found him and gave him my number, but I wasn't sure if he was actually gonna call. I'm glad he did! I'm smiling now, "Boy, it's been a long time! How you doin'?"

"I'm good, I'm good! Ay, Saint, what kind of shit you done got into? How long you been in the A?"

"Man, it's a long story...too long to talk about over this phone, but I'll get you caught up soon enough. But, yeah, I been in the A for about three or four months."

"And you ain't call me? Man, that's messed up!"

"Nah, it ain't like that. I been down here working, bruh'. I ain't even have time for my damn self! You still in the business?" I let that hang in the air for a minute. That's my boy, he already know what I mean when I say that. I ain't need to say anything more.

"Why? Wassup? Do I need to come out of retirement?"

"Only semi. I need you to do a lil' detective work for me. I'm lookin' for this dude named Ant. He's been known to be in the Bankhead area. He probably still with Starr, the girl he took from me."

"I'll hit the turf and keep my ear to the ground and see what I can come up with. What you want me to do if I find him?"

"Do nothing. I just kinda wanna know how he movin' and if the girl still wit' 'em. Another thing, he loves cocaine and strip clubs, that should give you a good start. He got a weakness for pretty women. Just find out where he livin' and who he be with. Can you do that for me? I'll make it worth your time, you already know that."

"Of course I can, bruh. But from the sound of your voice, this sounds kind of personal. So, if it's personal to *you*, then it's personal to *me*. You want me to move on that lil' situation if I find out somethin'?" OJ was sounding dead-ass serious.

"Naw, I got this. I owe him and her one. But thanks!"

"Listen, I'm gon' do that for you bruh, but you don't owe me nothing. It's all out of love, feel me?"

"Dat's real. I got you anyways bruh. Love."

"Love." We hang up. Now. My plan is in motion. I stay prepared. OJ should've been the person I called from jump, instead of Ant, but whatever, we here now...let's get this party started!

# CHAPTER 45

I'm in my 3rd month of rehab and almost all of the swelling is gone. Like planned, I'm ahead of schedule. I know half of that is due to Kelly, my awesome therapist. But the other half is due to my determination. I always knew that I had it in me. I've been blessed beyond measure. There's a difference between *wanting* to walk again and *having* to walk again. All I keep seeing is my boys' faces. A tear runs from the corner of my left eye. I sit up straight and wipe it away before someone walks in and sees me. I'm too tough for that! Soon as I do, the doctor walks in. "Good morning Stephon. How are you doing? Excellent, I hope. Look at your condition today compared to when we first got you as a patient three months ago."

"I'm doing great Doc, thanks for asking." I look him in the eyes, trying to think of the best way to say this, "Y'know, I remember when I was a kid, I used to hate seeing the doctor because they always gave bad news. But I actually look forward to seeing you!" He chuckles a little.

"That's good to know! Well, since you're in such good spirits, I may as well give you this other bit of news…"

"And what's that Doc?"

"All of the swelling has gone down and you've regained all feeling and movement in your toes and legs. We thought it would take six months to a year, but you're way ahead of schedule. Now, it's just learning how to walk again. We need to combine the movement with muscle memory. But I know you can do it!"

I got a big-ass smile on my face now. "Thanks for everything Doc. I know I can do it too. Let me ask you a quick question, when I go into Phase 2 of my physical therapy, can I keep the same therapist? I don't want anyone new, I'm used to her. She's one of the main reasons I got back so fast, in my opinion. She's really good." And Kelly *was* really good. She was so good that I didn't want her working with nobody else till I get myself 100%. I need her right now, more than anyone else. He replied, "I don't see why you couldn't have the same therapist. She's one of the best we have here, so I understand what you're saying. Let me ask her how she feels about finishing your rehab process, but I don't see a problem."

We have a few more words, then we shake hands and he leaves.

Again, I'm in the room alone with my thoughts. I've been in DeKalb County Hospital for a little over three months; the whole staff knows me and loves me. They love my energy and how I keep them laughing. I'm just excited that I may get the chance to work with Kelly for a little while longer, even though I plan on seeing her even after I'm walking again. It's fun working with her. She's even loosened up a little bit, and isn't as uptight. I can still smell her body spray. Pomegranate and raspberry never smelled so good! That fragrance is embedded in my brain. I tell myself that I am gonna marry her, even though marriage has never crossed my mind with any female I've ever been with before. That should tell you how serious I am! Kelly took the day off to handle a family matter that popped up and I refuse to work with anybody else, so I guess I have the day off, too. I'm stubborn. And a lil' jealous. I think me and her are alike in that way. I should ask her what her sign is. Hopefully she'll be back tomorrow!

# CHAPTER 46

The next morning, my eyes pop wide open as that certain fragrance hits my nose. I think I'm dreaming when I hear her say, "Hey sunshine!" I sit straight up in the bed and clear my eyes and see my Kelly, and that big, pretty smile of hers.

"Hey Miss Lady. Aren't you a sight for sore eyes? I thought I was dreaming!"

"Nope. It's me. You act like you missed me or something!" Her eyes flirt with me.

"Why? *You* miss *me*?" I said. "Don't answer that! I know the Doc told you the good news…"

"Yeah, he told me. And I'm glad for you. Time for Phase 2. But this is where it really gets hard; trying to get you back to where you were, but even stronger. I hope you're ready."

"Hell yeah, I'm ready. Let's do it!"

She helps me into the wheelchair, and I roll myself to the bathroom to wash my face and brush my teeth. Gotta get ready to sweat!

We leave the room and she takes the long way to the therapy room so that we can have some time to catch up; at least that's what I'd like to think. I ask her the same question that was on my mind from the night before, "Kelly, lemme ask you somethin', what's your sign? When's your birthday?"

"I'm a Sag. December 12ᵗʰ. Why?"

I knew she was a Sag! She was too cool to be any other sign. I knew it! I chuckled a little, and said, "I knew it."

She smiles, "Oh, OK. Well, when's *your* birthday?"

"December 1st! Fellow Sag baby! That's why we get along so well and that's probably why you like me so much! We're soulmates."

We both laughed at that. Then she said, "I bet you tell all the girls that."

"Nah, not all of 'em; only the ones that help me learn how to walk again." We laugh some more.

By this time, she's pushed me around the whole hospital before we finally get to the physical therapy room. I'm actually glad to see it this go-round! I can feel my lower body again, so I have a whole new purpose now! She helps me out the wheelchair and sits me on the mat to start our stretching exercises. We do this for maybe an hour. It feels real good to see my toes wiggling. The things we take for granted. I'm determined to go back to the streets stronger than before.

When she put me on the leg press machine, I already know my legs aren't gonna be at full strength, but I didn't know that they were gonna be straight-up weak! My legs are wobbling like an infant's legs; all rubbery and unsteady. But as long as you have a will, there will always be a way! I'm sweating bullets. I'm even getting frustrated, but not enough to give up. Kelly is pushing me harder than she's ever pushed before, and I like it. I *need* it. She is in my ear like a football coach, screaming and yelling, "Come on! Come on! You can do it! Don't stop now! Quitters never win and winners never quit!" The cheerleading goes on the entire time. So, now I'm tired, sweaty and getting yelled at, all at the same damn time! I guess this was all a part of me getting my motor functions back!

This goes on for another month and a half. I'm slowly getting back to my old self. I'm 'bout 75% of the way back to where I'm supposed to be, with the help of my special therapist! I'm actually out of the wheelchair now, and I'm using a walker to get around.

This particular day, Kelly comes by to check on me on her day off. I ask her if she would like to go have lunch with me. It will be my treat, plus, I need some fresh air. I haven't been away from this damn hospital since I was admitted, almost five months ago! She says yes. We take the elevator down to the main floor. She looks at me slyly, and says, "Let's walk!" So we do!

We walk maybe two blocks until we get to this lil diner called Charlie's. It was a really nice restaurant, but you couldn't tell from the outside! It's not run down; it just doesn't fit the dynamic of a downtown business. But Kelly says that she'd eaten there before and that their food is pretty good. It's sorta packed, so we grab a table in the back. We sit down across from each other and small-talk till the waitress comes to take our orders. It feels good to get out of that hospital and eat real food, plus I have great company!

"Thanks for joining me for lunch Kelly. And thanks for everything you've done for me."

"You're welcome. It's my pleasure, plus it's my job!" She flashes that slick lil' smile again.

"I forget you get paid for it. I thought you just liked me."

"Now why would you think that?"

*Because your eyes keep flirting with me*, I'm thinking, but what I say is, "Cause I'm a fool for love, I guess. Let me ask you something?"

"Go for it."

"You already asked me this question, but now it's time for me to ask you. Where do you see yourself in five years?"

She thinks for a second. "In five years, I'm try'na be the top physical therapist in the Southeast region. I'm try'na have my own practice and not work for the hospital. I love my job, but I love the people more."

"Good answer. Now, what about the relationship status?"

It's taking her longer than normal to answer. She finally says, "I guess I'll still be waiting for my Prince Charming to sweep me off my feet. No one has done it yet, which is why I'm still single."

"OK. Now…what kind of man do you like?"

We pause for a moment as the waitress comes to take our order. And then Kelly continues, "Well, I like assertive men, but not too aggressive. A man who knows how to take charge. A man who knows what he wants…"

I cut her off, "Sounds like me! But OK…so, what turns you off?"

"Oh, that's an easy one! First off, I hate a scary man.… also a cheating man; a lying man; a cocky man; a man who says one thing but does another; and last but not least, a man with no sense of humor!"

"None of them are me, so I'm good! You gonna love you some me!"

"Your confidence is off the charts for a man who's just learning how to walk again."

"I'll bounce back, trust me! Let me ask you somethin' Kelly…"

"You got a lot of questions! Go ahead."

I lean in kind of close; maybe two feet from her face and say, "How would you feel if I were to give you a lil' kiss of appreciation?" All of a sudden she's shy and looking everywhere except in my eyes. But she doesn't say no, so I decide to take charge of the situation. I grab the back of her head, lightly though, and guide her face toward mine. I can tell she wants to kiss me; she just needs me to show her. I'm assertive, but not too aggressive. Her lips were just as soft as I thought they'd be. And then I feel it; that spark…that flame. I know she feels it too. Her eyes are closed and she is breathing heavier. I have to play it off like I am cool, "So…how's the weather?" That breaks the moment and we both share a nervous laugh for a few minutes.

Our lunch comes and we eat and chop it up for another hour or so before heading back to the hospital. When we get there, she puts her number in my phone, thanks me for lunch, gives me a kiss on the forehead and tells me she'll see me tomorrow! *Seeds are blooming…*

# CHAPTER 47

After another two weeks of therapy, my legs were starting to strengthen. I still needed my walker, but I didn't require Kelly's assistance getting in and out of bed anymore. I was even taking four or five steps on my own. I had another hour before it was time for my therapy when my phone rang. It was my partner OJ and he had some news for me. The news that I had been waiting for.

"Wassup Saint?"

"What's goin' on O? This kinda early, even for you. You must have some good news for me?"

He chuckled a lil' bit. "Why you say that? I might of just called to check on a good friend? Is that so bad?"

"No. Not at all. I know one thing; you gonna live for a long time cause I was just thinkin' about you!"

"Is that right? How's the rehab going?"

"Pretty damn good. I'm about 75% of the way back to where I need to be. As soon as I'm 100%, you'll know about it! But, I'm walking on my own, a lil', right now. I'm just glad my legs work, to be honest. It's scary when you can't feel your legs. You see your life flash before your eyes. You go to thinkin' about what could've and should've been. Then regret starts to set in. But I'm over that now!"

"Man, I'm glad to hear that. We still got catching up to do. I know you a soldier and you'll bounce back 100%! But, ay…guess what Saint?"

"What's good?"

"I found him." He paused for about ten seconds, "*And the girl. They still together.*" He stopped talking and let that sink in. A cold chill ran down my spine. My right hand, that was holding the phone, started to shake. I wasn't scared; it was anger. I was pissed off! I was *that* much closer to the guy who tried to kill me; *my own cousin.* It took me about thirty seconds to snap out of it.

"What?" Even though I heard what he said clearly. I just had to buy myself another few seconds to get the words out right.

"I found that duck you was looking for!"

"Damn, you a life saver! I been dreaming about this day since I woke up in this hospital bed. You got all the other information I need too, right?"

"Come on, man; I'm a professional. I got everything."

"Alright good. Good! Now check this out, keep a loose tab on him. I need to be 100% first. This somethin' I gotta do on my own though, OJ. Don't do nothing. Just watch. Where you find him at?"

"Just where you said I would. It wasn't hard."

"Alright cool. Just keep doin' what you doin'. I'll be ready soon. I'm gon' take care of you when the time come, cool?"

"Alright. I'll keep in touch. Love."

"Love."

Damn I love it when a plan comes together! I got my ducks in a row and it was almost time for my Thanksgiving feast. The police came to talk to me months ago, after I was first shot. I gave them some BS story about me puttin' the wrong address in my GPS and I got lost. When I got out my truck, these three guys jumped out on me and tried to rob me. I ran and somebody shot me two times. I had no clue who it was. They brought some pictures of convicted felons in the area, but I couldn't pick anyone out of the lineup. It was dark outside; I couldn't see them! They believed me, I guess, because they never came back and questioned me again. I didn't want Ant or Starr in jail. I needed them on the streets; that's the only way real justice would be served.

Now it was time for me to call my girls and tell them the good news. First: I'm walking again and Second: I found those two traitors and in a couple of weeks, it would be showtime! I dialed Amanda's number and told her to put the phone on speaker, so they could both hear me.

"How my girls doin'?"

"We been doin' good. But we still need you out here with us!"

"I know, I know. I gave ya'll enough of the game to maintain for a couple more weeks till I'm 100%, right?"

"Yeah...you did."

"Listen...I found them."

I let that settle in. It took them about ten seconds before Trish responded, "So what we gonna do? I'm ready right now."

"I know ya'll are, but I'm not. I need a few more weeks to get my legs right, but I got my folks keepin' an eye on them. I know their every move. I know where their families live. I know where they get their haircuts at. I know what they gon' do before they do it. I got my end covered. But what I need from ya'll is to find that girl that ya'll used to dance with at the Premier. Have a sit down meeting wit' her pretty ass and tell her we need her for a mission. Ya'll know what to do."

Amanda spoke, "Oh yeah. I remember her. She would be good for this kind of job, too, cause she don't have many friends and pretty much just sticks to herself."

"That's why I want her. Make it happen. Set it up for another two or three weeks from now. Tell her she'll be paid well."

"Ok papi, no problem."

"I'll talk to you guys later. Love ya'll."

"We love you too."

I hung up feeling good. A lot was accomplished today. I smiled to myself because I couldn't wait to put this lil' play into motion.

# CHAPTER 48

Monday, 8am. Three weeks later…

That was all it took for me to fully bounce back to my old, strong, youthful self again. This is the best day of my life. I'm fully recovered from my gunshot wound and even though I'd probably be scarred forever, it would serve as a reminder. Kelly is so proud of me. I am proud of myself! She's already planning a little getaway for us, as soon as I get the doctor's 'okay'. I tell her that I have a lil' money put up, and if she could get a few vacation days, this trip was on me. I gave her a list of ten places that I wanted to see, and out of those, she picked somewhere that neither one of us had been; Paris. We'd leave the moment I have the doctor's approval. This would be the perfect opportunity for us to *really* bond and get closer.

I am officially released from the hospital and she is here to pick me up. My first question is, "Where do we go from here?" She doesn't hesitate, just smiles and says, "Let your seat back and chill. I got this." So, that's what I do. It's not easy for me to let someone else take control, but I keep forgettin' that she's a Sag, too, so it's natural for her. We drive for about thirty minutes till we pull up to this two-story, Miami-style condo. I don't ask where we are or who lives here. I'm just glad to be out the hospital! I follow her up the Victorian-style driveway to the front door. She digs in her purse, finds the key and opens the door. Guess we're home! She steps inside, with me following right behind her. This was the most beautiful place I've ever seen. You can tell, immediately, that she lives here alone. Everything is white and perfect. Then I hear a dog barking and a tiny, five pound yorkie comes running up to her. "Mommy's home!" She bends down to pet him. His name is Bentley, like the car, and he's looking at me strange. She reaches behind me and closes the door, then looks at me and says, "Welcome home."

She's smiling, I'm smiling…it's time for us to really get acquainted. I put my tongue in her mouth, and she isn't embarrassed this time. She grabs me and as we're kissing, I walk her backwards, towards the kitchen. She snatches my shirt off with one hand, and with the other she places my hand underneath her dress on her hot spot. She starts breathing heavier. I lift her on top of the kitchen counter and pull her dress and panties off in one motion. She unclips her bra and is totally naked in front of me. I can't believe how beautiful she is. Her nipples are hard, vagina wet. It's about to go down! She whispers, "It's been a while, so take it slow please."

"Just relax. I'll be gentle." I whisper back.

I start by kissing on her neck which leads me down to her breasts. First the left one, then the right one. Then I slide my tongue down her stomach right until I get to that special spot. She has both hands on the back of my head. She's sitting straight up on the counter when I spread her legs apart, and put my tongue to work. She is moaning so loud that the dog starts barking. I run my tongue in and around her clit till her juices start flowing. She's shaking and quivering. About twenty minutes in, she pushes my head back and slides off the counter. She pulls my pants down...then my boxers. She takes my penis and starts kissing it from the shaft to the tip and back again! It's in her mouth now and she plays with it for a good twenty minutes till she pulls me on the ground and pushes me on my back.

 "I wanna feel you inside of me," she whispers. She straddles me and slowly moves up and down, up and down on my dick. One orgasm, then another. I can tell it's been a while because she's really, really tight. I gotta slow down, take it easy on her. As a matter of fact, I let her take control this first time, I don't want to hurt her. I care too much for her to do that.

Over the course of two hours, we make love on the kitchen counter, the stove, the floor... even the refrigerator! We are consummating that bond I always knew we had.

From day one, I knew I could be the man that she told me she needed in her life. When we finished, I said to myself *I found the one I'm gonna spend the rest of my life with.* I knew, after that first time, that she was the one. We start putting our clothes on, and I say "Welcome home." We both start laughing.

As we are chillin' on the back patio, I figure this is the perfect time to let her know that tomorrow I'd be heading home for a few weeks to see my sons and my grandmother. I want them to know that I'm okay and I also want to see them before we take our vacation. I have something else to do, as well; I have to handle this lil' situation with Ant and Starr. But I want to make sure I'm fully recuperated before I take that on. The few weeks in Fort Lauderdale will be the perfect therapy for my body and my mind.

# CHAPTER 49

## Part Four: THE BIG PAYBACK

Four weeks later…

My first step is to get in touch with OJ. It's time for a face-to-face with my old friend. We plan to meet at the Starlite Café on I-20 and Confederate Blvd. in about 45 minutes. I'm wearing a dark jogging suit and a baseball cap that slightly conceals my face.

Kelly was already at work. She left me the keys to her other car - an all-black Infiniti Q35. I see she has good taste in many things! I hit the expressway. I haven't seen OJ in about four years. We met when we were freshmen and became instant friends. We had a lot in common. We were both from out of town, 6'4", and on the football team, before the streets started calling our name. We both are paranoid and have trust issues. Both of us only sleep a max of three to four hours at night, if at all. The last time we saw each other was when we were terrorizing the streets of Daytona while attending Bethune-Cookman. He fared a little better than me, though. I went to prison. He didn't. He eventually dropped out of school and moved to Atlanta. Since we've known each other for so long, we've picked up a lot of each other's habits; like always being early. We didn't like anyone beating us to the punch. They say the early bird catches the worm; well, men like us want to catch the worms, the crickets, the grasshoppers...hell, we even want to catch the other birds! We're relentless like that. So, I got to the diner within twenty minutes, only to find out that OJ was already there! I get out the car and see him looking at me though the front window. He comes out to greet me. We hugged and grab a table outside.

"My man, OJ. Wassup fool? What they do?" Still smiling, he says, "Slow motion, that's all. I can't complain, and if I did, who'd listen? Glad to see you walking again. They can't keep a good man down." "Thank you sir. I see some old habits never change," pointing at my watch.

"Oh, you talkin' about me being early? You know how we do!"

We share a nice little laugh together. "Remember when I said I was gonna call you when I was ready?"

"Yep."

"Well…I'm ready!" To show him how serious and how ready I am, I put an envelope with 15 grand in it, on the table. He takes the envelope and put it in his pocket.

"Well, let's get this party started then! I got two of my people watching their hotel room right now. Matter of fact, I keep somebody watching 24/7! This past week, they've been at Club 20/20 every day. I guess the girl must dance there. They been bringing different girls back to the room every night. I hope you got a plan."

"Of course I do! And tomorrow I'm gon' lay they ass to rest."

"That's real na'. So what else you need from me, you know I don't mind getting my hands dirty."

"Oh, I already know what type of grimy you is. We ain't just meet fool! But I'm good right now. I'll let you know if anything changes. You did a good job bruh', I appreciate everything. That's love."

"That's what real friends do. That shit hurt my heart when I heard about what happened to you, man. These dudes out here playing for keeps, and you need to do the same."

"I know. I got caught slippin'. But if you don't believe nothin' else, believe this, payback is a bitch." He looked in my eyes and said, "Say no more."

We pick up our menus and order us something to eat while catching up on our old college days. I tell him about my two sons and my new lady. He tells me about his kids and his old lady. We are just two old friends, reminiscing. Tomorrow is coming quicker and quicker. We finish up our meal, shake hands and I tell him I'll be calling him tomorrow night to get their exact location. We get up, give each other hugs goodbye and I tell my brother I'll see him again in the future.

# CHAPTER 50

I sit in the car for about ten minutes after OJ leaves, gathering my thoughts. The wheels are in motion, I just need my final aces in the hole; Amanda & Trish! They've been waiting on this call for weeks. It's finally time! I'm walking full strength and everything's back to normal, except one thing; I'm out the game. The old life I used to live, I can't do anymore. I'm in a relationship now, and that old life is old news. Even though I never forced any of the girls to do anything they didn't want to do, some people would still view it as wrong. I don't know how the girls are gonna handle the news. Amanda will probably take it the hardest since she's the closest one to me.

My next stop is Home Depot and then on to the exotic pet store. But first I need to call the girls and let them know I'd be by their place in about two hours.

Ring ring ring...

"Hey boo!"

"Hey Trish, wassup babygirl?"

"Nothing. Wassup Saint?"

"Chillin'. Check this out, I'll be by the apartment to talk to you girls in about two hours." I spoke quickly cause I really didn't have time for small talk. We can do that when I get there.

"Okay!"

We hung up and I GPS'd the Home Depot. The nearest one was in Stockbridge, about twenty minutes away. As soon as I got there, I picked up exactly what I needed: three shovels, two five-gallon paint buckets, ten bags of quick set mortar, ten pounds of cement and two gallons of pure lye. I push the shopping cart up to the cashier and it all comes to $287.52. I paid cash - no paper trail.

As I load up the trunk of the car, I call OJ to see if he knows where I can get a couple of opossums from; not many, maybe eight or so. Just like I figured, he has an uncle that stays near him that sells opossums, raccoons, and whatever other wildlife I need. I put in an order for eight opossums and for fifty of the biggest wood rats he had. I ask OJ to pay him for me; I'll reimburse him when I see him.

I'm on Highway 285-N, on my way to the girls in Bankhead. It takes me about forty minutes to get to the apartment. I've never been there before, but as soon as I pull up, it feels like home. I park the car, walk up to the door and knock.

"Who is it?" It sounds like Trish's voice.

"Saint."

I hear the dead bolt unlock and Trish pulls open the door and screams and jumps on me, kissing me and crying. I look around Trish and see Amanda. She walks toward me slowly, with one hand over her mouth, fighting back tears. She finally reaches me and gives me a hug and a kiss and says, "So you *finally* home?" We just look at each other for a minute. I am reunited with my girls. I finally step inside the apartment and close and lock the door. I take a look around...impressive. The place is hooked up and it's in a good neighborhood. They guide me to the living room, where we all sit down and chit-chat, just catching up.  After about 15 minutes, Amanda asks "When did you get out papi?"

"I got out the hospital a few weeks ago." Fuck it! There was no reason to lie. They both have a puzzled look on their face. Amanda then asks, "So where have you been staying?" I could see the jealousy in her face, "With that therapist lady, I bet!"

"As a matter of fact, that is correct. And that's another reason I wanna talk to you ladies." They both look at me and say, "What's going on?"

"A couple of things. I never lied to ya'll before and I ain't gonna start now. Me and the therapist, her name is Kelly, well...me and her are kinda together now, but I still love ya'll. The second thing is, I found Ant and Starr. I got my people watching their every move and it's time! Ya'll ready?"

Amanda spoke first, as usual, "First off, we love you too and we're happy for you and Kelly. And we couldn't wait for you to find Ant and Starr. Damn right we ready! We was just waitin' on you!"

Trish says, "I'm glad you're happy."

They did exactly as I taught them; they put their feelings and emotions to the side for the bigger cause. I like that! "Now, that's what I wanna hear," I said. "I got everything that we gon' need in the trunk of the car, outside. I got the shovels, buckets, lye and the cement."

Trish asks, "What we need all that for? Can't we just shoot 'em?"

"Nah...nah...that's way too simple. Where's the fun in that?" I do a lil' wicked laugh, and they both start laughing with me. "We gonna have some fun tomorrow. I need ya'll to pack up all of your belongings cause after this go down, I want ya'll on the move. I want ya'll to continue out west and don't look back!" They nod in agreement, knowing that

I wouldn't tell them anything wrong. "Oh yeah, before I forget, what's up wit' the girl, Passion, I asked ya'll to get?"

"Oh, we already got her papi! We sat down and talked to her a few days ago. She ready! Especially after I told her she was gonna be paid well. I'll even have her stay here tonight to make sure she's in place for tomorrow."

"Good thinking! Now, this is what I need from her: I need her to go to the strip club tomorrow night and be seen. I need her in her sexiest outfit. I want her to let Ant and Starr take her to their hotel room. We'll follow them in my car. Once we get to their hotel room, we get 'em. From there we send Passion on her way with her money. Then Trish, you get in Ant's car and follow us to the secret location. The rest is history! Got it?" They are smiling cause now they know the entire plan, but what they don't know is that I want their hands just as dirty as mine, so I ain't ever hafta worry about them ever snitchin'.

"Yep! We got!" Amanda said. Then, "Ooh, I can't wait!"

I tell Amanda to pop the trunk on the truck so that I can put all the stuff from Home Depot in it. I get up and give them hugs and kisses and tell them I'll see them tomorrow. It's on!

# CHAPTER 51

I could get used to waking up next to Kelly every day. As a matter of fact, I better get used to it! I gave up my other life for this one, and I don't have any regrets. And why would I? I got my dream woman and she got me. Everything's working out perfectly for me. Kelly's working overtime today, so she won't get back home until around 11 tonight, which will give me more than enough time to handle my business. Ain't no turning back now!

We sit down at the table and eat the breakfast I made for her: whole wheat toast, scrambled eggs and grits. I gotta make sure my baby got all her energy! I start washing the dishes and she grabs her purse to head out to work. She gives me a kiss and tells me she'll text me on her break.

I got a full schedule today. After I finish washing these few dishes, I'm gonna go and get the car washed. I also gotta call OJ to make sure he got the rest of the things I need to roast my duck. But before any of that, I need to call and check up on my kids. I dial Talia's number.

Ring…

She answers on the first ring. "Wassup?"

"What's goin' on?"

"I'm good. How are you doing?"

"I'm good. How's Zion?"

"Zion's doing good. He misses you already. Thanks for coming to see us. He's in school right now." "Oh shit, I forgot. OK, well just tell him that Daddy loves him, alright?"

"Alright."

We hang up. It didn't really make any sense for me to call Shonda since King was probably in school, too. But I just needed fresh energy around me today, so I sent her a text: "Tell King, Daddy says I love him, alright?" Ten seconds later she texts back:" Alright, I will."

Now, I'm set!

# CHAPTER 52

I hate not being able to let Kelly in on my plans, she's my backbone; we tell each other everything. Well...*almost* everything. I can't tell her what's goin' down tonight because I know how she feels about this type of thing. I hate to keep secrets from her, it almost feels like I'm cheating on her, but this is something I have to do for *me*. When she asks me what happened and how I got shot when we first met, I told her the same thing I told the police and investigators. It wasn't exactly a lie...just a less detailed version of the truth. Plus, that was when we were just getting to know each other. I couldn't tell her *everything*, I didn't trust her like that yet. I was still figuring her out. In the middle of my thoughts, she texts me: "I miss you and I'm thinking about you. I'm glad you're in my life." This woman knows how to soften me up! At times I feel like she is just finessing me, but in actuality, she is just being herself. I never met a woman like her...ever! I respond to her text: "I miss you too, boo boo. Believe it or not, you saved my life. I found my soulmate when I found you." Oh yeah, I got a way with words, too. And all of mine are true. Two things in life my grandmother taught me at a young age: #1: Never play with a woman's weave and #2: Never play with a woman's heart! When I was ten years old, a woman tried to kill my uncle. She stabbed him twelve times in the stomach. I will always remember that.

Me and Kelly have only been living together for about a month, and I was out of town for half of it, but I can already see how she is. I got comfortable with her very quickly. She made me feel at home. She never used the word "*my*", and always made me feel like what was hers, was mine. This type of woman don't come a dime a dozen; they are priceless. You can't buy this type of woman either, you gotta earn her. And over the course of those six months in the hospital, that's exactly what I did!

As a matter of fact, I think I'll drop by the hospital today and surprise her with some lunch! That's what she makes me wanna do - be a better me. But right now, I gotta call OJ to make sure he got my stuff!

Ring ring ring...

"Yo! Wassup bruh?"

"Yo! What's good? You got everything I need?"

"Sure do! You comin' to get it now?"

"Where you at? I'm on my way!"

"I'm at my uncle's spot now. It's off of 285-S toward Macon. I'll send you the address."

"Cool. See you in a few."

# CHAPTER 53

After I took the car for a quick hand wash, I surprised Kelly and brought her a quick bite to eat. I brought her a chicken caesar salad from a nearby deli we'd been to a couple of times; Rubio's. I got to her office and found out she was busy with clients. I was kind of glad cause I didn't really have time to stay and eat with her today. I was in a rush, but we'll have a lifetime of eating together so it's alright! I left it on her desk and told her that I'd call her later. It was time to go meet OJ. After a 45-minute drive, my navigation told me I was approaching the farmland where OJ's uncle stayed. I saw his car as soon as I pulled in. This was actually my first time on a real slaughterhouse-type of farm. As soon as I got out of the car, OJ came up to me and we shook hands. We walked close to the barn and his uncle, Ben, was waiting for us inside. Me and Mr. Ben shook hands. I call him Mr. Ben because he's about 60 years old. Me, OJ and Mr. Ben walk to the back of the barn where all the animals are kept and that's where he has my packages waiting for me! He has three cages for me. Two cages have the eight opossums with razor sharp teeth and the other cage has 50 wood rats that are about two pounds apiece. They are ready! I lay down a blanket on the back seat and put two cages on it; the other goes in the front seat. I go back and give OJ the $500 I owe him. We shake hands and I tell him that I'll call him tonight. OJ only has one job left... to watch the hotel and let me know what time Ant and Starr leave.

I'm riding down 285 on my way to the Blue Ridge Mountains to survey the area cause, in a couple of hours, it was showtime! After an hour of driving, I am finally there! The area is huge. I turn into the forest and drive about 10 minutes in, where I find the perfect location! I write down the directions to how I got there, so I'm sure not to get lost and that I would be 100% sure of how to get back. I park the car, get out and put flags as markers on several of the trees. I open the car door and take out the opossums and rats. It's getting dark outside, it's now 6:45pm, and the sun is going down. I have to hurry up and finish what I'm doing. I took out the flashlight and popped the trunk. I put on my latex gloves and grabbed some rope and made a knot. I throw half of the rope into the tree and let the front end of the rope catch a branch and fall down to where I was on the ground. I tie all three of the cages together into a knot and hoist them into the air so that the forest animals won't eat them. After I finish this lil' task, I take off my gloves and throw them on the passenger's seat, turn off my flashlight and back out. I know exactly how to get back to this same location so I'm good! I'm on my way back from Blue Ridge when I decide to swing by Amanda and Trish's apartment. I wanna burn some time over there for a few. And have the girls nearby when OJ calls. I call Amanda.

Ring ring ring…

"Hey."

"Wassup Ma?"

"What's good?"

"Ya'll home, cause I'm on my way over there."

"Yeah, we home, come on!"

"Alright I'll be there in 30 minutes!"

"Ya'll got Passion wit ya'll?"

"Yeah, she in the shower. I told you I got you."

"Alright, I'm on my way!"

Things are falling into place. It's almost time for me to bake this cake.

Amanda and Trish come through for me again! Those two ain't let me down yet!

# CHAPTER 54

I pull up at the girl's house and it's now 8:15 pm. It was almost time. I'm getting excited. I get out the car and knock on the front door. Amanda answers. She gives me a hug and lets me in. Trish is on the couch. She gets up and gives me a hug. I ask where Passion is and they say she's getting out the shower. I sit in the living room with the girls till she comes out. Five minutes later she enters the room with only a towel wrapped around her. She is just as beautiful as she was the first time I seen her at Club Premiere. She's a tall Puerto Rican woman, curly brown and blonde hair. She is perfect for the job. Before she gets dressed, I ask her to have a seat on the couch next to me while we talk. I start off by saying,

"I remember you from a couple of months ago. You remember me?"

She nods her head. "Yeah I remember you."

"OK, good. I know they told you a lil' bit about what's happening but I'm gonna give you the full run down, alright?"

"Alright."

"First off, you're gonna go to the strip club where the girl Starr works. Wherever she is, Ant's close by. I want you to be all over Starr; make her feel like she's the most beautiful woman in the club. Don't even look at another woman. When she on the stage, go up there and tip her all night. I want you to proposition her for sex, tell her you'll pay for it if you have to! If she say anything about her dude, tell her you want both of them. They'll love that! Can you do that?"

"Piece of cake!" she said.

"And another thing, I'm gonna give you $5000 after I get them in the car with me. Cool?" I ask, knowing that it should be cool.

She says, "Hell yeah that's cool!" then she laughs.

I show her the envelope with the $5000 in it, just to show her I'm serious. Then I pull out another envelope with $1000 in one dollar bills and hand it to her and say

"Now this is your tippin' and drinkin' money. Don't be cheap. You gotta sell the shit outta this. You gotta be a good actress. You want them to take you home, but don't worry;

we gonna be following ya'll the whole time, and when you get to their hotel we'll take it from there. Alright?"

"I ain't worried! I got this!"

"And another thing, don't worry about them coming back for you or no retaliation later cause you ain't gon' see them no more after tonight."

"I know. I ain't worried."

"Good. Good. I ain't gon' let nothing happen to you, I promise. Now go get dressed cause it's almost time."

She took the $1000 and walked to the room to get dressed. That's when I yell out "Wear your sexiest dress please!" She yells back, "Of course!" I like this girl already! She better be glad that I'm out the game cause I'd probably put her on my team.

After about 30 minutes of small talk, my phone rings and it's OJ. His people just called him and informed him that Ant and Starr was on the move; probably headed to the club. OJ and his people was following but we should get going. I thank him, hang up the phone and relay the message to my girls; "It's showtime. Time to go!"

Me and Passion ride together in Kelly's car while Amanda and Trish ride together in the truck. The girls follow me, but not too close. I call Amanda and tell her to go to Ant and Starr's hotel and wait for me to follow Ant back to the room. I don't want him to spot my truck. I also tell them to make sure they have their guns with them. I text Trish the address to the Hilton hotel on Wilshire where they are staying. After the girls follow me for about ten minutes, they get off the highway headed for the hotel. Pawn move #1. Now that I got a few minutes to talk to Passion, I give her the usual pep talk. I tell her to get comfortable, I got her back. I lift up my shirt and show her my chrome 45 Desert Eagle, and let her know that *he* has her front.

We finally get to the club. I see Ant's car and my eyes get wide. I'm excited. I'm in the same vicinity as the dude that tried to kill me. I gave Passion a kiss on the cheek and tell her to make it happen!

# CHAPTER 55

10:42 PM.

I park the car about ten cars away from Ant's. It's a packed night at Club 20/20! He wouldn't notice this car even if I parked it right next to him; it's nothin' to him. Since I couldn't go inside the club, OJ did me the favor of sending one of his guys inside to give me the play-by-play. OJ gave his guy my number so that he could call me when he spotted my girl. I told him what she was wearing: a red, tight-fitting dress with a split running up the side and some red stiletto heels. It was gon' be hard to miss her. That's why I wasn't surprised when five minutes after Passion walked in the club, he called me. He must have had me on his blue tooth because he sounded crystal clear, despite all the music playing in the background.

"Hey Saint?"

"Yeah, wassup?"

"Can you hear me?"

"Loud and clear."

"Well, I just spotted your girl and she the finest woman in here! Everybody watching her, including Ant and Starr!"

"Perfect!"

I sit in the car, patiently waiting for an update. And then it comes.

"Here we go. Your girl just came from the bathroom and went straight to the bar. While she's waiting for her drink, two different men approach her trying to buy her drinks and talk to her; she brushes them off! She gets her drink and walks around the club very slowly glancing at all the girls. It seems like more women than men are trying to approach her. They love her in here. I guess cause she's new and she's hot! Hold up one minute...I think she just spotted Starr in the corner giving a customer a lap dance. She's walking over to them. Now she's stopped right in front of Starr and whisperin' something in her ear. She pulled away and went into her purse and took out, what looks like about a $100 in ones and throws it in the air so that the money rained down on Starr and her customer. Nice move! She so disrespectful! It must have been a good move cause dude got up and left and Starr didn't even look back at him. She just pulled your girl down by the arm and made her sit in the seat and started dancing on her. Damn, they going at it! They over there kissing! Hold up, I think the dude Ant just walked up to the girls and whispered something in Starr's ear!" He paused for a minute.

I ask him "What's going on now?"

He says, "Starr got up and went to the stage, I guess it's her turn and your girl's right behind her. Hold up…Ant just walked up to her and they talkin' now. They laughing. Ant just got her another drink. They're both sitting at the stage. Your girl just went in her purse and pulled out a bunch of money. She makin' it rain on Starr. Ant is in her ear. They laughin'…"

This play-by-play dialogue went on for about another thirty minutes. It seems like the three of them are getting along very well, which is exactly what I wanted. Now, I just hope she is talking to them about bringing her back to the room with them!

It's 11:33pm and Kelly just sent me a text. She must've just got in from work and is wondering where I am. I text her that I'm with my buddy OJ and that I'd be home in a couple of hours. Then I get back to business. OJ's guy is still on speakerphone when he says, "I don't know what your girl just told Ant and Starr, but Starr just went to the back like she leaving work for the night. Ant and your girl are at the bar. It looks like they waiting for Starr to come out, so they can bounce."

I say, "Are you sure?"

"I'm positive. So get ready."

With that being said, my blood pressure starts to rise. I get hot. I even start to sweat. It's happening. The time has come!

OJ's guy starts talking again, "The three of them are walking outside right now, alright?"

I say, "Gotcha!"

Before I hang up, he says, "Good luck."

# CHAPTER 56

I let that statement hang in the air for a couple of seconds before I snapped out of it. I had to call the girls real quick.

Ring ring ring...

Amanda answered, "Hello?"

"Hey baby girl, ya'll get ready. We should be there in about 15 minutes. Hide the truck real good, alright?"

"Alright."

The wheels are set in motion. All three of them come outside the club, laughing and holding hands, just having a good ole time! They hop in Ant's car and drive off. I wait, maybe thirty seconds before I take off in the same direction, being careful not to be too obvious. I keep several car lengths behind them, driving at least ten miles per hour slower. We've been on the road for fifteen minutes and in about two more exits, we'll be there. I send Amanda a text that says, "They'll be there in five minutes. Get ready." She texts back: "We stay ready!" *Perfect.* I got the a/c on high, so why the hell am I sweating? They get off the exit to the hotel and a few seconds later, I do too. We are almost there. *Three more minutes.* The stop light turns green; it won't be long now. *Two more minutes.* I pulled out my Desert Eagle and kiss it one time. *One more minute.* I think about my kids, and how these people tried to take their father away over some damn money. I get mad all over again. They park at the hotel, on the pool side. I find me a spot on the opposite side of the building. I get out and run around the building, and as soon as I get there, I see Amanda and Trish standing over Ant and Starr with their guns at their heads. Passion goes and gets in the back seat of the truck. Check!

# CHAPTER 57

Every dog has it's day...

I go over to the truck and make sure Passion is okay. I tell her she did a great job, go into my jacket pocket and give her the envelope with the 5Gs in it. I tell her that this is where we part ways. I tell her to catch a cab home because we have business to handle. She gets out the truck, puts her envelope in her purse, gives me a hug and says, "Thanks. Anytime you need me, call me!" She waves goodbye to the girls and walks in the opposite direction.

Now back to Ant and Starr. I pop the back of the truck and get out the duct tape and rope. I put my latex gloves on and walk over to where the girls were. I tape Starr and Ant's mouths tight; there won't be any screaming tonight! I take the rope and tie together their hands and legs, and throw them in the back seat of the truck. I tell Trish to get in the passenger seat and Amanda to drive. I direct her to Blue Ridge Mountain, which is about twenty minutes away. The girls seem more excited than me at what's about to go down. They are smiling and laughing the entire time. I love these two psycho women! They have no clue what I have waiting in the mountains. They probably think I'm just gonna shoot 'em and bury 'em. Nah...I got some whole other plans, but these two are crazy enough to like it.

We are now in the area. I tell Amanda to make a left once I see the marker that I left for myself. Then I tell her to drive ten minutes in, at two miles per hour and we would run straight into it. I see the flag that I left on the side of the ficus tree. I tell her to stop. We are here!

They're looking around, confused. I tell Amanda to keep the lights on. I get out the truck and tell Trish to pop the back so we can get started. I look over at Ant and he's crying like a two-year-old. Me and the girls start laughing. I look at them and say, "Ya'll ready? I need one of ya'll to help me dig and the other one to watch them."

Trish immediately says, "I'll dig!"

"Let's do it!"

I get two shovels out the back and we start digging.

The first hole we dig is about five feet deep and six and a half feet wide. This one is for Ant. Starr's new home is about five by six. After we finish digging, I go to the passenger door to take Ant out first. Before I throw him in the hole, I take the tape off his mouth. I kinda want to hear the bullshit and the pleading. As a matter of fact, I *need* to hear him scream and beg for his life. I know it's sick but...oh well! I rip off the tape and roll him in the hole.

"Please cuz, I'm sorry. Don't do this cuz. I was high on them drugs. I'm sorry! Please, please don't kill me cuz!"

"Man, shut up and quit all that damn whining!" I tell him as I walk back to the truck to get Starr. It was her turn now! Oddly enough, I'm having way too much fun. I get her out the truck and rip the tape off her mouth. She starts screaming and crying and carrying on like Ant. "Please Saint, I'm so sorry! Ant made me do it. I didn't want to, he threatened me! Please! I'm so sorry. Give me another chance!" Then she really pissed me off with her next line, "I know you're a God-fearing man, Saint. What would Jesus do?" This made me laugh even harder. Me and the girls are laughing so hard, we are in tears. I tell her, "So now you wanna bring God into it? Where was God when ya'll shot me and left me for dead?" Before she could answer, I threw her ass in the ditch. "Ain't no fun when the rabbit got the gun!" Me and the girls are standing over their gravesites, laughing. Then I pull out my surprise. I untie the rope and lower the three cages down to the ground. My girls look on in amazement and Trish says, "This just keeps getting better." They come closer to the cages and see my hungry animals who haven't eaten in days. I tell Trish to get me the bottles of honey from out the back of the truck. I told her to pour the honey all over Ant's body, including his face. Make sure she gets it everywhere. I tell Amanda to do the same to Starr. Don't miss a spot! They take pride as they do it. These girls are just as sick as I am! After about ten minutes, the adrenaline starts rushing through my body. It is time!

"Now, I don't know who propositioned who about setting me up, so ya'll are both equally guilty." They are both blaming each other. It wouldn't have mattered either way cause they both shot me. I just had to decide which one to give their surprise to first. Me and the girls play 'Rock, Paper, Scissors'. Ant lost. Guess he's first!

I grab the two cages filled with the eight opossums and toss them all on Ant. He is *really* screaming and crying now! Me and the girls stand, staring down at him and laughing at how much he's carrying on. After about fifteen minutes, it's time for Starr's surprise! Of course, she hears Ant screaming, but she has no clue as to why. She's about to find out! I dump fifty of the biggest wood rats I've ever seen in her ditch. She starts screaming like crazy as they start eating holes in her face. "No Saint! Please! Stop!!!" I blocked out their cries a while ago. I was numb now.

I guess the opossums work fast cause after about fifteen more minutes, Ant isn't screaming anymore; at least fifty percent of his body was eaten away. About ten minutes later, Starr is in the same predicament, except her bite marks are smaller. In the end, the damage is still the same. She'd already stopped screaming, but every now and then she let out a little moan.

I knew it was officially over for Ant when I saw an opossum crawl out of his stomach. There were guts all over the bottom of the ditch and they were eating every last bit. I never turned away. I watched the entire time. The girls did, too. The rats took a little longer on Starr. It was about 1:30 in the morning, and they still probably had a few hours before they were through with her. But I had to get home to my lady; it was time to speed this process along. I told Amanda to get me the lye from out the back of the truck. I poured it on Ant's body and it dissolved everything, including his bones. It even killed the opossums. After pouring three gallons in his ditch, the only evidence of any occurrence was a shoe string. Starr met the same fate as Ant. I didn't feel any remorse, neither did the girls. The lye turned everything into a liquid which soaked into the ground. Nothing was left. Job well done! I was happy that everybody got their hands dirty.... literally and figuratively. We did it. We hugged and kissed goodbye. *Checkmate. Game over.*

# CHAPTER 58

As soon as we put the last scoop of dirt over the two grave sites, we pack up the truck but before we take off, I tell them I need a moment to myself. They sit in the truck as I walk back toward the ficus tree to make sure nothing is left behind.

On the way back to the hotel, I ask the girls what they plan on doing. Amanda seems to have it all figured out. She says her and Trish are gonna keep living and working together, and they still plan on heading out west, since the idea was already planted in their heads. By the time we finish our conversation, we are already back at the hotel. They drive me to Kelly's car and we all get out and talk for a few more minutes. I ask them if they have any regrets. They both answer, *No, not even one*, at the same time. Everything happens for a reason. I look both girls in the eye and say, "I have another surprise for ya'll." Trish says, "I think we've had enough surprises for today!" I tell them I'm serious and

I pull out two house keys. They are for a three-bedroom condo in Las Vegas, almost fully paid for. I also pulled out the title to the Escalade, that I have signed over to Amanda. I explain to them that I'm doing this because I love them and don't want them to struggle for anything out in Vegas. Amanda looks at me strange, then says, "You keep saying *y'all* and not *us*. So, I guess this mean you're leaving us?" I couldn't lie to them. I never could, even if I wanted to. "I'm not leaving ya'll, ya'll leaving me! I want ya'll to go on to the next phase in your life. I've given ya'll all the necessary tools that ya'll need to make it." Trish side-eyes me, "It's that damn therapist, ain't it? She came and took our man!" We all laugh. Then I say, "Oh yeah, I forgot to tell you guys, there's a safe built into the wall of the condo." I hand Amanda a sheet of paper with the address and the code to the safe. They start smiling. Especially when I tell them that there is $24K and some jewelry in there. I have a connection in Vegas that, over the past couple of months, has been helping me set all of this up. They both hug me and start crying. We cry together, cause in actuality, we are all heavily indebted to each other *for life!* We would always be bound together because of the things that only *we* knew. Before we let each other go, Trish whispers in my ear, "We have a surprise for you, too." They give each other a knowing look. Trish hands me the key to the safety deposit box that they had been using while I was in the hospital. "We left about 38K in there for you to start your new life. We had a feeling that you were gonna do something like this, so we wanted to make sure that *you* were starting out on the right foot, too. We know you love us, and we know you love her, too. We just wanna see you happy." They give me another hug and start crying all over again. We all have a feeling that this is gonna be our last time seeing each other. Some words just don't need to be said. I tell them to head out to Vegas tonight, and when they get there, sell the truck and get a new ride. One last hug and me and my girls part ways. "Love you," they said.

I say back to them both, "Love" …

# CHAPTER 59

I use the drive back to Kelly's to dry my eyes and clear my head. That chapter of my life is closed and there is no going back. I am on my way back to the new love of my life. It's about 2:20 and I know she's probably worried. But the good thing about her is she gives me breathing room and doesn't smother me.

I got back to the house and park the car in the driveway. I get out and walk to the front door. I'm still dirty and sweaty from digging those ditches, so I leave my shoes outside the door. I use my key and walk in. I know Bentley heard everything; I'm just waiting for him to come around the corner barking. But he doesn't. He's just sitting there watching me. It's like he knows. I rub him on the head and make my way to the kitchen. When I switch on the light, I can see Kelly asleep on the living room couch. The television is still on. Look at my baby looking all peaceful. She has absolutely no clue what kind of night I had! I don't wanna wake her yet. I creep upstairs to the bedroom and take a quick, hot shower. I'm trying to wash away all the sins of the night. All the dirt I'd done; I ask the Lord for forgiveness. Hey! If that's what helps me sleep better at night, don't judge me!

I put on the pajamas that she bought me and spray on a little of the *360* cologne; she loves it. My plan is to go downstairs to wake her, then carry her back up to the bedroom, but she is sleeping so sound and looked so comfortable, I just curl up next to her on the sofa. She must have sensed me near her, cause she lets out a low moan and opens her eyes a little to make sure it's me. Then she slides over so I can lay comfortably beside her. I kiss her on the forehead, and she whispers to me, "Glad you made it home safe." No more words need to be said. That's all I ever wanted and needed from my woman; to just trust me and know that I'll never hurt her. That's why I don't mind changing my entire life for her. Because of how she is. I never even met a close second.

# CHAPTER 60

The alarm on my phone goes off at 8:30am. I push snooze and then five minutes later, it goes off again. Kelly is still asleep on my chest. I kiss her on the forehead. "Good morning beautiful."

She opens her eyes slowly, "Good morning baby." I ask if she's hungry and she nods yes. I get up and go to the kitchen to make some eggs and bacon. While the food is cooking, we catch up on yesterday's events; it's been a good 24 hours since we've spoken. She's exhausted from the double she pulled and glad that her vacation officially starts today. She's taken three weeks off, which is great news to me. "That's good bae. So now you get to hang with me for almost a whole month! And the doc says I'm okay to travel out of the country, so Paris here we come!"

She starts smiling, and gives me a kiss. "Since you like surprises, I have one for you. I'm late." I'm totally confused because I could swear she *just* said that her vacation starts today. "Late for what, bae?" She gives me a look, like *are you for real?* I know...sometimes I'm so fuckin' slow She starts smiling and patting her stomach. "Oh shit! Are you serious?" I lift her off the ground and spin her around. This is some of the best news I ever heard in my entire life. *Everything is falling into place...*

# EPILOGUE

One year later...

My baby girl is now three months old. How time flies! Her name is Zariyah and she's the second love of my life, after my wife, Kelly. We've been married for almost a year and life couldn't be better. Zion and King are staying with us now, as well. Their mothers understand that I need some time to really bond with my sons. I'm not trying to take them away, I just need some *us* time and they understood that, for which I'm appreciative. Now, my family is complete.

My barber shop business has picked up dramatically in the last six months. Honestly, it's doing a lot better than I thought it'd be. This type of success during the first year is unheard of, especially in the beauty industry.

Tomorrow is me and Kelly's one-year anniversary, but I have a surprise planned tonight, just to throw her off. She's a Sagittarius, like me, so she thinks she knows everything!

I'm gonna cook her a Porterhouse steak, parsley potatoes and I got a bottle of her favorite *1999 Marcassin Vineyard Pinot Noir*. She's working till eight tonight, so I have time to slow cook the steak, just how she likes it. I have the candles ready and made a playlist of her favorite slow songs.

Zariyah is with her grandmother for the week and King and Zion are staying over their friend's house tonight. Everything is going perfect when I hear my phone beep; indicating that I have a voice message. That was kinda strange because I didn't even hear it ring! I open my phone and hit the voicemail button. It's Amanda. There's a two-minute message saying that she's in the Atlanta area and has something very important to discuss with me. She's wondering if we can meet up for lunch. I think about it for a few minutes before I decide to call her back. This is a major decision for me to make. When I sent the girls to Vegas one year earlier, it was with the intention of never seeing them again. Not that I didn't think about them from time to time; it's just that my life is different now. I'm married; I have my three kids with me...

That one-year hiatus now seems like just a few weeks. All the old memories start playing out in my mind. I can't help but laugh at some of the good times we had. Then the laughing stops and I get serious. I start to think of that *other* incident. Could this call be about that? Did something happen to Trish? What if they didn't get rid of the truck like

I told them to, when they got to Vegas? My mind is racing now. I wanna know. I *need* to know! Why'd she have to call me today, right before my anniversary? This girl has horrible timing…

# PREVIEW:
## "THE WORLD I ONCE KNEW"
# CHAPTER 1

I return her phone call, like she knew I would.

"Amanda. Wassup? You alright? Where's Trish?" I'm in the middle of my kitchen, the steaks are already marinating. I'm prepping the meal, but I have to return this call. I haven't heard from either of them in a year!

She answers, "Yeah, I'm fine. Well…not really. I need to talk to you. Is there any way that we could meet up for lunch or something?" She lets that question hang in the air like it was skydiving. I know that meeting up with the girls won't be a good idea, but we have too much history for me to brush them off like I don't know them. Hey, there's nothin' wrong with having lunch with some old friends, right? "Sure. Where you wanna meet?" I say nonchalantly, like this isn't a huge moment for us. What the hell does she want? Why now? Seconds later she responds with, "Remember that diner we used to go to off I-10 North and Peachtree? I'll be there in an hour. Is that cool?"

"Yeah, I remember where that place is. I'll see you in an hour."

I know exactly where that diner is. Me and Kelly ate there three weeks earlier when we were downtown doing some shopping for the baby. She's expecting me in an hour so, as always, I'll leave now so I can be there early. Some things never change. I'm just paranoid, I guess. I leave the steaks in the sink cause I plan on coming right back. I throw on a white t-shirt and some shorts, then hit the door.

Driving down I-10, I couldn't help but get a feeling of déjà vu. Even though this moment wasn't exactly like one I'd had before, it felt the same. I got domesticated being a husband and a father and I was okay with that. My business was now the #1 new small business in the Atlanta metropolitan area. I even made the *Black Weekly* magazine's front page, twice. I see my kids every single day. I'm also King's & Zion's little league coach and I'm President of their PTA at school. Me and Kelly might have had one disagreement, if that. We get along very well. I'm successful in my own right and I can't complain at all! So why am I ten minutes away from looking at my past with eyes of the future? Only God knows...

# CHAPTER 2

I arrived at the spot thirty minutes earlier than scheduled, to be surprised by Amanda sitting outside at one of the tables smoking a cigarette. When did she start smoking? I guess a lot has changed in a year. Since I notice her before she sees me, I think I'll circle the building to scope out the scene. I pull around the back and there are only three cars parked. I'll park back here and walk in through the back door. I taught that girl too much, now she's arriving at destinations before me! I can't be mad though, she learned from the best. I walk through the back door and everything looks normal. I speak to a couple of the waitresses while I stroll through making my way to Amanda. There are a few regulars in there that I remember from the last time I came. So far, so good. I walk out the front door and I see Amanda reading a newspaper, taking a drag off her cigarette. I wonder how long she's been smoking. From the looks of it, you'd think her whole life. And where's Trish? She never actually said if Trish or anybody else was with her; I guess I was just assuming.

I walk up behind her and whisper in her ear, "Is this seat taken?" She never even looks at me or even glances in my direction when she says, "Yes, I'm waiting for someone." Maybe three seconds pass before she catches on to my voice. She looks at me, drops her newspaper and jumps on me, wrapping her legs around me like one of my kids would do! I missed her playfulness. As a matter of fact, I've missed *her*, but there are a lot of questions that need to be answered. We hug for what seemed like thirty minutes. We kiss. Then we hug some more, before she finally calms down. I look in her eyes and see tears. I hope they are tears of joy. She dries her eyes, then says, "Have a seat. How the hell have you been papi?" She seems genuinely happy to see me and I am glad to see her, too. So much has happened since they've been gone, I don't know where to start or how much to tell, so I just let it flow and wait to see where my intuition leads me. "I been doin' good. You know me, I always seem to find a way. I'm happy. So, how about you? How are you doing? And where's Trish? I was expecting both of you." She's still smiling as she starts answering me, "I'm doing good. Well, *we're* doing good." She isn't smiling as much now. "Trish is doing fine. I knew you'd ask about her when you saw me without her."

"Of course. You girls are my babies."

Then she got serious, "That's the reason I'm here. Our 'baby' Trish has made it big time."

I'm lost. I have no idea what she means, so I just come out and ask, "What are you talking about?"

She puts her hand in mine and says, "Trish is in a relationship with Jose Montoya. Do you know who that is?"

I really don't know, but I guess it's someone from the west coast.

"Nah, not really. Am I supposed to?" I give a dismissive shoulder shrug like, 'Who the hell is *he*? Does he know who *I* am?' That's what I say in my head, anyway.

She responds, "He's the second biggest Mexican drug dealer on the west coast. And he's in love with our sweet Patricia. They've been dating for about three months." She's looking at me like I am supposed to jump for joy or something. I mean, I am proud of her for landing a man of that stature, but what does that have to do with me? Me and Amanda could have had this conversation over the phone. Now I'm really confused, so I just say, "Good for her. Glad to hear she's happy." And I mean it. But since I know Amanda, I know there has to be more, and of course.... "There's more. Jose has been beating Trish since they met. He's obsessed with her. She doesn't even live with me anymore. I mean, we speak every day, but she lives with him now. But that's not all...." She left my mind wandering for a short time, then she speaks again, "He keeps 30-50 kilograms, and at least ten million dollars in a safe house and Trish knows where it is. She has the pass code to the gate to get inside. She went there with him a couple of days ago and saw him put it in and now our girl's ready to take it all. So...what you think about *that*?"

Damn Amanda. You just dropped a real live bomb on me. I was content with living the right way, now I got a decision to make. I got a lot of people depending on me. I got Kelly and my three kids on one side, and on the other I got Amanda and Trish, who need me as well, but for their own selfish reasons. Life is full of decisions. I really wanna direct her to someone who can pull off the job, without me getting involved at all. Someone like my main man, OJ. But I know Amanda wants me, myself, on the job. I owe them. I can't tell them no. *And*, he was physically abusing her. That might have been the one thing that helped me make up my mind. Now all I had to do was make up a good lie that would buy me about two weeks out of town. My mind was made up in that instant. I said, "Fuck it! Let's do it!"

# CHAPTER 3

The ride back to my house was a long one. I had to come up with a good enough lie that wouldn't make Kelly suspicious. I hate lying to that woman, especially since, to my knowledge, she's never lied to me. I didn't want to give her a reason not to trust me. I just knew she wouldn't approve of me packing up and leaving for a week or so with a female friend. That don't even sound right.

Kelly was actually a pretty cool girl. I'd like to believe that if I told her what I was actually going to do, she would send me off with her blessing. But that's just me; trying to justify having to lie to her. Amanda's been back in my life for all of fifteen minutes and already got me on the verge of committing a robbery, kidnapping and deceiving my wife! I sure hope this doesn't backfire. I can just hear Kelly now, 'You have a successful business. You've stayed out of trouble for over a year! This time, last year, you were trying to learn how to walk again. We don't need the money. I don't get it. You wanna risk it all trying to rob a Mexican drug lord?' Even when I play this out in my head, it sounds stupid. This is the kind of shit that happens when you feel indebted to people. Just like I owe my wife loyalty, I feel like I owe the girls loyalty. Kelly could leave me at any time and I would guarantee that Amanda and Trish would take me back with open arms. And it's not that I think she would, it's just that me and the girls have a different type of bond. I keep thinking back to when I first got with them, I made them both the same promise. I said I would never let anyone hurt or harm them, and I meant that. The money and the drugs are just a bonus.

This is a big job and I have to handle it the right way. First, I'm gonna need some help. In a situation like this, there's only one person in the world that I can bring in with me; that's the juice man, OJ. All he has to do is bring in two or three people that he trusts and we'll have a complete team. The money will be divided equally, four ways. Me, OJ, Amanda and Trish. And then we'd all kick in to pay OJ's guys. But that's just me thinking ahead. I'll sleep on it tonight and we'll see what tomorrow brings.

I get back home at 4:45. My baby gets off work at 8. That leaves me about three hours to get this kitchen smelling like a 5-star restaurant. I can't tell if I cook really, really good or if my wife just loves the hell out of her husband, but it really doesn't matter as long as I can keep a smile on her face...

THE END